Masquerade

NEW YORK TIMES BESTSELLING AUTHOR

K.M. SCOTT

WRITING AS GABRIELLE BISSET

Masquerade is a work of fiction. Names, characters, places, and events are the products of the author's imagination. Any resemblance to events, locations, or persons, living or dead, is coincidental.

Published in the United States
ISBN-10: 1941594190
ISBN-13: 978-1-941594-19-3

Cover Design: Cover Me, Darling

Interior designed and formatted by

www.emtippettsbookdesigns.com

Adult Content: Contains adult sexual content

Masquerade

Annelisa Fielding has had the blessings of wealth her entire life, thanks to her industrialist father. However, there is one thing even he can't give her: a title. So he arranges a marriage between his daughter and the Earl of Swindon, Thornton Sutcliffe. As long as his future bride is a virgin, the Earl will tolerate the marrying down because in return for taking Annelisa as his wife, her father will pay off his debts. Everyone wins, as far as the men are concerned, but Annelisa wants more out of marriage than a title and is willing to wait. But time is running out. If she doesn't find some way out of the marriage and fast, in one month she'll become Lady Annelisa Sutcliffe.

The solution to her problem? Count Nikolai Shetkolov, a diplomat in the service of the Tsar and stationed in England. Single, powerful, and sexier than any man Annelisa has ever laid eyes on, Nikolai is the perfect choice to help a young lady lose the one thing her odious future husband prizes most. But Annelisa will have to watch out or she may get more than she bargained for with Nikolai.

Masquerade

One

1878

Annelisa concealed herself behind an enormous Oriental vase as she stood outside her father's study spying on the meeting that had just begun inside. She knew exactly who he spoke to. Her future husband.

"My Lord, it is a pleasure to have you in my home."

"Yes, I'm sure. Let's dispense with the pleasantries and get to the situation at hand."

"Yes, of course."

Frustration boiled up inside Annelisa. How could her father be so obsequious and to Thornton, Lord Sutcliffe, no less? Cursing her father's old fashioned ways, she struggled to listen as the two men carefully decided the particulars of her future.

"My daughter will make you a fine wife, my Lord. She's had an excellent governess who has educated her well in many subjects, including French and Latin. Her intelligence is always cited as one of her finest qualities, of which she has many. And she is one of the most beautiful young ladies in all the county."

"Then why does she remain unmarried at such an advanced age?"

Annelisa blanched at Lord Sutcliffe's painfully rude question. To her, twenty-five wasn't an "advanced age" and the disdainful tone of his question offended her. And he had a lot of nerve to refer to anyone's age as advanced. He was twice her age!

"What I need to know, Mr. Fielding, is one very important fact. Is she a virgin?"

"My Lord?"

"You heard me. Is she still intact? It's of the utmost importance that any wife I take be a virgin on our wedding night."

"Yes, yes. I understand, my Lord. I can assure you that my daughter is still as pure as the day she was born."

"Good. Your family will benefit a great deal from this marriage, Fielding."

Frozen in place, Annelisa listened to the indelicate discussion of her virginity, part stunned and part furious. Lord Sutcliffe's claim that her family would profit because of her marriage was only a half-truth, and she knew it. Despite his title as Earl of Swindon, he was nearly penniless. He'd squandered his family fortune in risky business ventures and what some gossiped was a gambling problem. By marrying her, he'd receive the benefit of her father's substantial wealth, thereby solving his financial problems.

It was a situation common in industrialized England. Lord Sutcliffe had a title and some possessions but little wealth. Her father had tremendous wealth from his chemical factories but no real social prestige. The one thing that could remedy both men's deficiencies?

Her becoming Lady Sutcliffe.

But Annelisa didn't want to marry Thornton Sutcliffe. In fact, she didn't want to marry any man. While all her female cousins and friends had long ago found husbands, she'd been content to remain with her books and artwork. Yes, it was true that at one time a few years earlier she'd believed she would marry, just as it seemed every other young English woman did. Now, however, the prospect held no appeal for her, and the idea of marrying a fifty-year-old earl obsessed with her virginity practically disgusted her.

"Then we have a deal, Mr. Fielding?"

"Yes, my Lord."

"Make sure she's ready in a month from now. And I'll expect those payments to begin then also."

Before she could make a hasty escape, her father and Lord Sutcliffe exited the study, and she found herself face-to-face with them.

"Annelisa, you remember Lord Sutcliffe, the Earl of Swindon."

"Yes, Father." Turning to face the man she'd just been promised to, she smiled and feigned politeness. "My Lord. It's lovely to see you again."

Nothing could be further from the truth. As she

examined the man who stood sullenly staring at her, she saw a thoroughly unappealing person. Thornton Sutcliffe was short, pudgy, and appeared almost as old as her father with his salt and pepper hair and overgrown sideburns. That he had the manners of a barnyard animal made him even worse.

With a grunt and a nod, he turned to her father and began walking to the door. Disgusted, Annelisa watched him leave, wishing she'd never have to see him again, and stalked into her father's study.

"I know what you're going to say, but let me remind you that I'm still your father," Andrew Fielding said as he sat in the leather chair opposite Annelisa's.

"Then as my father, how can you marry me off to that...that....cur! Please reconsider, Father."

"You know in the long run this will be a wonderful thing for you. By marrying him, you'll become a Lady. And you'll help this family in ways I never could, even with all my money."

"He's odious! Did you see the way he reacted to me? He only wants this marriage because of your money. He cares nothing for me."

Annelisa watched as her father shifted in his seat and hoped she was getting through to him.

"It's an advantageous match for you, dear. It's not as if there have been many offers of marriage in the past few years. Lord Sutcliffe can provide you with security, social status..."

"What about love, Father? Is there to be no love in my life?"

Andrew Fielding grimaced at the truth his daughter refused to ignore. Annelisa knew she was being difficult, but if it took that to change her father's mind, she would happily cause him discomfort.

"It's not always possible for one to have love in a marriage, my dear Annelisa."

"Then am I to be sacrificed on the altar of expediency and usefulness?"

Annelisa saw she wouldn't win this fight. Frustrated and frightened by the life that lay before her, she struggled to hold back the tears. Unless she could change either her father's mind or Lord Sutcliffe's, she would be married in a month and her life of misery without love would begin.

"Please understand, dear. We can talk about this later, but now I have an appointment with the Russian minister."

Knowing this was her cue to leave, she rose and made her way out to the hallway where her father's appointment waited. Annelisa forced a smile onto her face in respect for Nikolai Shetkolov, the Russian minister who'd become close to her father in the months since he'd arrived on assignment in Britain.

"Good afternoon, Count Shetkolov."

"Good afternoon, miss. How are you today?"

"I am traded, sir."

Nikolai's face registered his confusion at her remark. "I'm afraid I don't understand, miss. I find sometimes my English is woefully lacking."

"No sir. I apologize. I was being intentionally confusing. I am fine, thank you. My father waits for you."

"Thank you. Enjoy your afternoon, miss."

Nikolai bowed in respect, and she returned the courtesy. He left her alone in the hallway with her misery, but she wasn't ready to give in just yet. If she couldn't find a way around marrying the distasteful Earl of Swindon, then she didn't deserve to be considered intelligent.

And if there was one thing she prided herself on, it was her intelligence. There was a way out of this. She was sure of it.

"Nikolai, you're a welcome visitor today—a respite from my troubles. Sit. May I pour you a drink?"

"Thank you, yes."

As he took a seat in the chair in front of Andrew Fielding's desk, he saw that his friend indeed did look beset by problems. His normally genial grin was absent, replaced by a furrowed brow and frown, and the tone of his voice had an air of melancholy.

Nikolai took a sip of his drink, letting the alcohol slide down his throat before he spoke. "What bothers you today, my friend?"

Andrew groaned. "Do you have a daughter, Nikolai?"

"No, I have no children," he answered with a chuckle.

"Be happy. And when you do, if you have daughters, don't indulge them as I have mine. You'll regret it for the rest of your days."

Sighing heavily, Andrew Fielding leaned back in his chair. "You've met my older child, Annelisa. She's a lovely girl, the apple of my eye. Maybe that's why I spoiled her. She's had the best governesses money could buy, but they did their job too well."

While his friend stopped to take a drink, Nikolai wondered how there could be a problem with Annelisa Fielding. Beautiful, charming, intelligent—she was exactly what any man could want in a wife.

"She's twenty-five now, although I wouldn't say that's an advanced age. But it's not even that she's still on the shelf at twenty-five. The problem is she's not what young men want."

"If I may say so, then they are blind."

"Oh, it's not an issue of beauty or grace. It's her intelligence. She's just too smart. I always thought she should have been a man.. As a man, she'd have the world by the tail. But as a woman...that's a different story."

Nikolai saw the frown deepen on his friend's face and knew his problems were more than a daughter with above average intelligence. Something more was bothering him.

"It's a father's job to see that his children are taken care of. You want them to have good lives, secure lives. Sometimes that means making difficult choices, but that's how it must be. So I've arranged a marriage that will ensure Annelisa is secure for the rest of her life. In one month, she's to marry the Earl of Swindon."

That explained why Nikolai had seen the earl walking from the house, his face in its typical full scowl. Always a surly man, Thornton Sutcliffe seemed an unlikely husband for a woman blessed with so many gifts.

"Needless to say, my daughter is less than thrilled

about the arrangement. She doesn't understand what this marriage can do, Nikolai. She'll be Lady Annelisa Sutcliffe. For all my success and money, I could never give that to her."

Nikolai sympathized with his friend. Many British industrialists felt trapped in a bourgeoisie status, millionaires with tremendous influence but never as high on the social ladder as those of the peerage. However, the idea of Annelisa bound to that bore for the rest of her life seemed a poor trade for a step up in society.

"And I have no answer for her when she asks me if it matters that this isn't about love. Young women today seem to think love is paramount in marriage. Silly romantics!"

"I feel certain she'll understand soon enough. As you say, she's a wonderful daughter and a smart young woman."

"I hope you're right, my friend."

Andrew sighed and Nikolai considered the marriage he believed was made just a few feet below heaven.

Annelisa lay across her bed, her arm covering her eyes. "Cecile, think. There has to be a way."

"You don't think father will do this to me, do you? I couldn't bear being stuck with an old man!"

"Cecile!" Annelisa sat up and glared at her younger sister.

"I'm sorry! It's just so awful."

"That's exactly why we need to figure out a way to

make the honorable earl not want me."

Cecile sat down beside her sister, puffed her cheeks, and blew the air out in frustration. "What if you became big and fat? Men never like that."

"In one month? I don't think even Pippa could make enough pies to achieve that."

"Could we make you uglier?"

Annelisa leveled her gaze at her sister and squinted her eyes.

"I didn't mean that you're already ugly! Don't look at me like that. You know what I meant!"

"I know, but this isn't helping. I don't think Thornton Sutcliffe would care if I got fat or ugly. As far as I can tell, he barely noticed I'm even human."

Annelisa fell back onto the bed in disgust. Cecile meant well, but they were getting nowhere. She was missing something right under her nose.

"Do you know anything about him? Oh, Anne! How could father do this?"

"I know very little of him, and what I do know, I don't like a bit."

"Other than his shortness, stoutness, and surliness, what else do you know that could help you?"

Annelisa buried her face in a pillow. "Cecile, there's nothing else to know. He's odious."

"Oh, don't cry! There's got to be something that will make him call off the marriage."

The two sisters remained silent until Annelisa sat bolt upright. "I've got it! I know what I have to do!"

"What? Tell me!"

"You must promise you'll tell no one, Cecile. No one can know what I'm going to do."

"I promise! Now tell me!"

"The earl seems to think it's of vital importance that I'm a virgin. So all I have to do is not be one."

Cecile leapt to her feet in shock at her sister's implication. "Annelisa Fielding, you can't! It's improper!"

"What's improper is that in this day and age a woman is still traded like cattle. Relinquishing my maidenhead is a small price to pay for my freedom."

"I don't know about this," Cecile said as she began to wring her hands.

Annelisa rose to face her sister. "I need to know you'll keep my secret, Cecile."

Her sister hesitated a moment but then nodded. "I promise I won't tell another soul as long as I live."

"Good. Now I just need to decide who will be my comrade in arms. Any suggestions?"

"You can't do that with any of the men we know. It would be a scandal."

Pacing, Annelisa nodded in agreement. "I know. There must be someone who would be willing to keep our coupling a secret."

"Perhaps you can find someone at the Stewarts' masquerade ball tomorrow night. There are sure to be many possible men attending."

Annelisa stopped and considered her sister's idea. The season's first masquerade ball would be perfect. Everyone would be wearing masks, and if she wore her hair differently, her choice wouldn't know it was her.

"But most of the guests are from our social circle."

"Not everyone."

"Annelisa, who do you have in mind?"

"Someone who is respectable, honorable, and best of all, soon to be leaving Britain."

Cecile grabbed her sister's arm to stop her from pacing. "Who?"

A broad smile lit up Annelisa's face. "He's perfect. I just hope he's not too honorable."

"Annelisa! Who?"

"Count Nikolai Shetkolov."

"Father's friend?"

"Yes." Annelisa saw the shock registered on Cecile's face. "What's the problem?"

"Do you even know him?"

"What do I need to know? He's an appealing man, always charming, obviously intelligent as he's a diplomat for the Russian Tsar, and if I'm not mistaken, he told Father he would be returning home soon."

"But isn't he a bit older than you?"

"Cecile, I'm not choosing a husband. I'm choosing a lover for one night to eliminate the one thing the Earl of Swindon believes is worthwhile about me."

"I'm worried. What if something goes wrong? What if you become pregnant?"

Annelisa cradled her sister's face in her hands. "Don't worry, dear sister. I'm an intelligent woman. I'll find a way to prevent that from occurring and secure my freedom all while keeping my identity from the good Count Shetkolov."

"I hope so."

Annelisa laid out her plan to her sister and secretly prayed she'd be able to pull it off. She had to.

Two

Nikolai Shetkolov arrived to the Stewart mansion punctually at seven o'clock. He found a scene as festive as any he'd seen in his months in Britain. Champagne flowed freely from twin fountains shaped like swans in the enormous dining room, and tables of fine dishes and desserts from around the world ringed the room. The Stewart family had made its fortune in the railroad boom, and with their considerable wealth, John Stewart and his wife Alice had traveled the world. Evidence of their globetrotting could be found on each overflowing food table. Nikolai recognized the dish of caviar on a far table and slowly made his way toward it as he kept an eye out for his host.

Everything about the Stewarts was big, from the mansion they lived in, to the superb chandeliers that hung in the middle of the dining room ceiling, and even to the man himself. Nikolai spied him making his way through the throngs of people who milled between the dining and ball rooms. As the portly man reached him, he extended his hand to greet the Russian.

"Nikolai! It's wonderful to see you! But Alice will be disappointed you aren't in costume."

As he shook John Stewart's hand, Nikolai searched the room for his wife. Equally as corpulent, Alice Stewart possessed a personality that many found difficult to disappoint. He, however, had to draw the line at dressing up in costume and parading around in a wig and mask as most around him did.

"I will do my best to make amends, John. A diplomat on assignment from the Tsar himself shouldn't be found dressed as a famous actor or a long dead king."

John slapped him on the back and let out his trademark deep belly laugh. "So serious, my friend. Come, let us find Jacobs and Josephson so we may talk business. We'll leave the partying to the rest."

After a half hour of performing his diplomatic duties in the service of Russia, Nikolai was ready to enjoy some champagne and the company of the revelers. As he stood filling his glass at one of the fountains, he recognized Andrew Fielding and his family entering the ball.

"Nikolai, how are you tonight? And no costume! Oh, the joys of being a bachelor," his friend joked as he shook his hand.

"It looks like you escaped the fate of others here, Andrew. You're still recognizable. Josephson is dressed as a sheik, and I swear you wouldn't know it was him if he didn't speak first. Your military costume hides little of you."

"It's very nice to see you again, Count Shetkolov."

Bowing to Eleanor Fielding, Nikolai said, "Pardon my manners, Mrs. Fielding. You look lovely tonight. As do you, Miss Fielding. But where is the other Miss Fielding tonight?"

"She's home, sick to death about her impending marriage to the Earl of Swindon, Count."

Nikolai struggled to stifle a smile at Cecile Fielding's candor and instantly saw the look of shock and displeasure come over her father's face. It was obvious Andrew's home life hadn't improved yet.

An awkward silence hung between the four until his wife graciously excused her daughter and herself, leaving the men to talk candidly.

"I'm sorry to hear Annelisa is still unhappy, but as I said yesterday, I truly believe she'll come around."

His friend rolled his eyes. "I do hope so, Nikolai. I hate to see her so miserable. When we left, she was in her room crying."

Nikolai sympathized with him, even if he disagreed with his choice of husband for his daughter. He'd seen firsthand the politics of marriage back home and secretly dreaded the day he might be forced to marry a woman merely because her lineage improved his own family's position. He should count himself a lucky man if he were to be married to someone like Annelisa Fielding.

"Excuse me, my friend. Let me rejoin my wife and Cecile. We'll speak later."

"Of course. Enjoy your night."

As he watched the room fill, Nikolai looked around at the women, finding none particularly appealing. Too many seemed the copy of every other woman in Britain.

How wonderful it would be to meet someone new tonight.

Annelisa's plan had been successful so far. It had been nothing to convince her parents of her inability to attend the ball because of her devastation over her impending nuptials. The distress on her father's face had tugged at her heart for a moment, but just the memory of his conversation with the earl cured her of any sympathy for his sadness.

Now, as she walked up the steps to the Stewart mansion, she scanned the entrance to see if she needed to overcome one last possible obstacle. She'd intentionally arrived late, hoping to slip in unnoticed as the rest of the guests enjoyed themselves, but if the hosts were still greeting people at the door, her plan might be dashed before it had a chance to succeed.

Luck was on her side this night, and she simply walked through the unguarded front door without a question asked. Now it would begin.

She saw him the moment she entered the main hallway. Much taller than most of the guests, Count Nikolai Shetkolov stood out with his light blond hair and chiseled features. Annelisa thanked God he'd chosen to attend the ball out of costume, solving yet another potential problem. Despite his stature, he wasn't the only tall man in attendance and if he'd been masked, she may have had to suffer through a number of conversations before she found him.

A quick glance in the antique carved and gilded mirror in the entryway ensured her that her white gown showed just enough skin as it sat off her shoulders while her shimmering white and silver mask covered the top half of her face perfectly. One deep breath and she was ready.

Casually, she approached him, confident her wig and mask concealed her true identity. However, just in case, she'd decided to add another layer of deception: she would affect a French accent, thankfully perfected through years of study of the language.

Perhaps I'll even speak some French if the situation calls for it, she thought, smiling.

He stood alone near the entrance to the ballroom, almost as if he were waiting for someone. All she had to do was make him interested in her and seduce him into joining her in some secluded spot nearby. Taking another deep breath, Annelisa willed away the butterflies in her stomach and reminded herself she had to succeed if she wanted to keep her freedom.

In her most alluring voice, she began. "Monsieur?"

He turned toward her and immediately she registered that he appeared different this night.

"Madame?"

"Mademoiselle, monsieur."

"Pardon moi, mademoiselle."

Annelisa was impressed by his accent. While his harsher Russian accent tinged his speech when he spoke

English, it was absent as he spoke French.

"No need to apologize, sir," she answered in a heavy French accent.

"You speak English?" he asked, his Russian accent obvious once again.

"Of course! We are in England."

As they spoke, she studied his face for any sign he was interested. In just a short time, she saw she'd piqued his interest.

"Allow me to introduce myself. I am Count Nikolai Shetkolov, diplomat for Tsar Alexander II."

Annelisa extended her gloved hand, and he bowed to place a kiss on the back of it.

"And who are you, mademoiselle?"

"I am the goddess Aphrodite, of course!" she teased.

Nikolai smiled. "No, I meant what is your name."

Annelisa had decided to use the name of a woman her governess had told her about—a French woman she'd known when she was a child.

"Violet Moceanu."

"It's a pleasure to meet you, Miss Moceanu."

"Are you enjoying yourself, Count? You don't dance?"

Annelisa watched him change as a stiffness overcame him.

"Not particularly well, my lady, but I will make an exception for you."

Behind her mask, Annelisa beamed. This was going to be even easier than she'd hoped.

"Perhaps later. For now, I prefer to enjoy your

company this way."

She watched as relief washed over him and his body relaxed. "I think I'd like to take a walk outside for some fresh air. Would you care to join me?"

"Absolutely, Miss Moceanu."

Taking her arm in his, he guided her through the library to the outside. As they strolled around the well-manicured Italian gardens famous to the Stewart mansion, they made conversation while Annelisa's eyes scanned the area for the place she'd bring her plan to fruition.

Just the way he spoke to her as if she were an intelligent being impressed her. She'd made a good choice in Nikolai, but as they continued to walk the mansion's grounds, she worried he might be a little too respectful to do what she needed him to do.

Subtly, she began stroking his arm with her free hand and then slid her gloved fingers inside his sleeve to touch his wrist. Even through the fabric, she felt the heat of his skin and sensed his pulse quicken as they continued their conversation.

She was sure he was interested. Now if she could induce him to make a move, she'd willingly oblige him and achieve her goal.

Stopping behind a large hedge out of the view of the other partygoers, she looked up at him and moistened her lips. Fear thrummed in her veins as she waited for him to act on her signals. What if he was too honorable to help her complete her plan? For a long moment, she wondered if she would fail as the thought of marrying

Thornton Sutcliffe made her heart sink.

Nikolai touched her mask and she quickly grabbed his hand to stop him.

"No."

"How am I to give you what you've been telling me you want if I can't see your face?"

"The mask must stay."

Despite his obvious confusion, her requirement didn't deter him. Gently, he pressed his lips to hers and kissed her. Annelisa's heart pounded against her chest at the thought that this was her first real kiss. Suddenly, fear raced through her. Was she doing it correctly? Would he know she was inexperienced in this, and therefore, in what she hoped would follow and end their tryst prematurely?

As she worried about these things, Nikolai dropped his head to her neck and softly planted kisses near her collarbone. In a hoarse voice, he whispered, "Moya milaya" against her skin.

The effect of his kisses surprised her, and an unfamiliar ache began to throb inside her. She pulled his head closer to her, weaving her fingers in his thick hair, and pushed her body to his, only intensifying the ache inside.

Each touch of his lips, each dart of his tongue against her skin excited her more. Her effect on him seemed equally arousing, if she was judging correctly the hardness that pressed against her body.

Sure she couldn't withstand much more, she pulled him back up to kiss him and timidly, out of curiosity, stroked her hand over his pants where her fingers felt his hardened cock. Suddenly, fear paralyzed her. What waited for her beneath his trousers—what would soon take her all-too-important virginity—felt enormous under her fingertips.

He whispered "Moya milaya" again, this time in a voice edged with need.

"Yes."

Annelisa wasn't sure what to say. It seemed that every bit of intelligence she so prided herself on had evaporated from her mind, leaving only a strange mixture of fear and desire to guide her.

His hands moved quickly to lift her dress, and at the first touch of his fingers on her thighs, the breath caught in her throat. His kisses stole the air from her, and she felt lightheaded. In seconds, he moved his hand to between her legs, cupped her sex with his palm, and groaned.

"Unfasten my trousers and use your hand on me."

Annelisa followed his order without a thought and soon had her fingers around him. Just touching his erection, with its hardness of steel but the softness of silk, took her breath away once again. Unsure, she slid her fingers over its top and felt a dampness.

As she reveled in the experience of his stiff cock in her hand and the effect her movements had on him, he slid a finger through her sex past a place she would have begged him to touch again if she could speak or even think clearly.

"Oh," she moaned against his lips.

"You like that? Do you like this?"

As the last word left his lips, he slid his finger into

her and began gently stroking its tip against her virginal walls. The invasion, coupled with the gentle circling of his thumb on the spot he'd touched before, sent waves of pleasure through her.

Frantically, she tugged at his hair near his nape as he continued his sweet assault. Nothing she'd experienced before in her life had ever made her feel like this. Her legs felt like they hadn't the strength to keep her standing if his strong arms released her. Every stroke of his finger made her want more—more of him, more of this.

She wanted to make him feel as good, so she became bolder in her touch, running her hand the full length of him from base to tip. With each stroke, his kisses became more passionate, more desperate for her.

Finally, he slid his finger out of her and tore her hand from him. "Violet..." he groaned and lifted her onto his cock. Holding her to him, he slowly pushed into her tight body, taking what another man prized above all else about her.

He filled her completely and stilled to allow her body to stretch as it took him all in. When her body relaxed around him, he retreated from her only to plunge into her again and again. Each thrust was accompanied by a grunt that seemed to come from deep inside him.

Annelisa held him tightly, her hands pressed against the back of his neck, as he rode her for what seemed like forever. She'd prepared herself for this—she'd read as much as she could find about sex, memorizing names and positions along with every physical detail and description books had offered.

But nothing had made her ready for what her body was experiencing.

Nikolai panted next to her ear as every thrust into her inched him closer to release. Frantically, Annelisa remembered she hadn't taken any precautions against pregnancy. She squirmed and bucked against him to release herself from his hold, but this only seemed to increase his passion.

"No!" She couldn't let him finish inside her!

"Yes," he groaned as he pulled her tightly to him. "Yes, yes..." he said as he plunged into her for the last time before he stopped and buried his face in the crook of her neck.

Annelisa felt the hot liquid flood her insides as his cock pulsated inside her. She'd done it. She'd lost her virginity and ensured her freedom from a loveless marriage to the dreadful Earl of Swindon.

But now she had to accept the very real fact that she may have just allowed Nikolai to impregnate her, sealing her fate once again. For if she were with child, she would be forced to reveal her deceit and marry him.

For all her intelligence, she hadn't planned on this.

Tenderly, he kissed her while he pulled out of her. Placing her on the ground, he covered himself and then reached for her mask.

"Now I must see my love's face after what we've just done."

"No!" she cried as she turned to run away.

Nikolai caught her by the hand to hold her, but as he grabbed her, she slid her fingers out of her glove and fled. She turned back once to see him still watching her, stunned that the woman he'd just made love to was running away.

By the time Annelisa arrived at her carriage, she was out of breath, her head spinning. She'd accomplished what she'd set out to do, but she feared she may have gotten more than what she'd bargained for.

"Tell me everything!" Cecile whined as she climbed into bed across from her sister. "I've wondered all night."

"First, tell me if Father or Mother suspected anything."

"Nothing. Father is upset that you're not happy, but I heard neither of them say a thing about you all night, even when Count Shetkolov asked about your absence. I made sure to mention how devastated you were about the marriage, just as you said to."

Annelisa smiled. At least that part of her plan had succeeded.

"Now tell me!"

"Everything went just as I planned," she lied. "I arrived and immediately saw him standing alone. It was like fate was smiling her favor on me."

"You know, Annelisa. I studied him carefully tonight. He's quite attractive with those pale blue eyes of his."

"Cecile, we're not engaged. Stop talking like he's taken the earl's place."

"Did I say that? I just noticed he's very handsome."

Annelisa shrugged. "Be that as it may, it matters none to me."

"Fine. Then tell me what happened next."

"I began speaking to him in French, and he responded in French but with no Russian accent. It's strange, but he sounds entirely different when he's not speaking English. There was no hint of his accent at all."

"Really?"

"Yes. Then I got him to join me outside in the garden where we walked and talked."

"What did you talk about?"

"Many things. He's quite intelligent, and I think he found me to be the same. We discussed the Stewarts' Italian garden. He told me about some real Italian gardens he saw when he lived in Rome as the Russian attaché to Italy a few years ago. He says the Stewarts' garden is very authentic looking."

Realizing how dreamily she sounded as she recalled their talk, Annelisa quickly changed the subject. "Then I gave him the signal that I was interested in more than simple talking."

Cecile's face expressed a combination of fear and curiosity. "What did you do?"

"I slid my hand underneath his coat and shirt cuff and caressed his arm."

"Oh, Anne! I can't believe what you're telling me! You're so brazen!"

"Not brazen. Brave. Father and the earl gave me no choice. I had to be fearless if I were to keep my freedom."

"So then what happened? I can barely wait to hear!"

Annelisa frowned and put her finger to her mouth. "Shhh. Lower your voice. I don't need Father or Mother hearing this."

Cecile took her sister's hands in hers and squeezed. "I'm sorry. You're right. It's just that I can't help myself. This is more exciting than anything I've ever heard."

"So after I let him know I was interested in more from him, we did it."

Annelisa sat back on her elbows and watched her sister's face change from curious to shocked.

"Did it? Tell me! There has to be more to sex than simply calling it IT."

As she listened to her younger sister's plea, she wondered how much she should tell her. Their mother had never told either of her daughters anything about sex. Prim and proper, Eleanor Fielding was the definition of old-fashioned. Annelisa couldn't imagine her even thinking of doing what she and Nikolai had done just hours earlier.

Everything she and Cecile knew about what a man and woman did in bed—or in the garden—together had been gleaned from books she kept carefully hidden away. Cecile had always been a less interested student of their knowledge, Annelisa suspected out of fear, so she knew even less.

How much should she tell her? Should she go into detail about how painful the experience had been while at the same time creating the most delicious sensations in her?

"Annelisa, you promised. How am I to know about these things if you don't tell me? Father's certain to see me married any day since I'm nineteen now. I need to know what to do."

"Okay, but don't get frightened. I'm sure it's much better between a man and woman who are in love...and in a bed. He touched me down there with his fingers, and it felt wonderful."

Annelisa felt foolish calling it "down there," but something told her it had been the graphic terms pussy and cunt found in her books that had caused Cecile to turn away from them.

Her sister's eyes grew as wide as saucers. She stammered, "Down there? With his fingers? Wonderful? Really?"

"Yes. It was wonderful."

"What about when he put his thing in you?"

Annelisa chuckled. She'd call female parts "down there," but she drew the line at calling his a thing. "Cecile, it's a cock. Or a prick, if you prefer."

Cecile waved her hands as if to make the two words her sister had said go away. "Whatever. How did that feel? Was it wonderful too?"

Annelisa sat up. "Not exactly. It was a bit painful, just as I read it would be."

She'd also read an average man was around five to six inches in length and easily encircled by a woman's hand. Obviously, Nikolai was an above average man, she concluded.

"But you feel fine now?"

Quickly, Annelisa sought to allay her fears. "Yes, I'm fine now. Best of all, Cecile, I'll be released from the dread of a marriage to Thornton Sutcliffe, the Earl of Swindon, and remain a free woman—a woman who can choose if and when she'll be married and to whom."

"How will you face the count when he comes to the house again knowing what the two of you did?"

Annelisa lay back on the bed. Facing him would be easy. He had no idea the woman he'd made love to was anyone other than a Frenchwoman named Violet Moceanu.

"Only I know. He doesn't even know what the woman looked like. I never took my mask off, so it won't be a problem."

Cecile fell onto the bed and hugged her sister tightly. "Oh, Annelisa! You're so brave. I don't know how you did it. I could never be like that."

"Yes, you could. And if father tries to marry you off to some old man you don't love, we'll just have to do the same for you. I won't let him do that to you."

Cecile sat up, her face full of terror. "Oh, no! What if he tries to marry me to that awful Earl of Swindon now?"

Annelisa patted her on the knee. "The earl won't want to have anything to do with either of us when he realizes my precious virginity has been taken. Even if he did, we'd just find you your own Nikolai to solve that problem."

Cecile calmed down and kissed her goodnight. "I

love you, Annelisa. If only I could be as clever as you."

Smiling, Annelisa hoped she had been as clever as her sister believed. For now, though, she'd revel in her victory over old fashioned paternalism and worry about everything else later.

By noon the next day, Annelisa was eager to give her father the news of her deflowering. She'd accepted that he would be furious, but the prospect of a loveless marriage to a man twice her age was much worse than the temporary anger of a father.

Business kept Andrew Fielding out of the house until mid-afternoon, but soon he was back in his study and she had to wait no longer.

Peeking her head into the room, she smiled at him as he sat behind his desk. "May I speak to you, Father?"

Andrew Fielding's face lit up in happiness. "Of course, Annelisa. Please come in."

She took a seat across from him and smiled in return. "Thank you, Father."

As he began to speak, he reached over the desk and took her hands in his. "Annelisa, I know you've been very cross with me, but I'd like to explain why your marriage to the earl is so important."

"That's what..."

Her father cut her off and continued. "Dear, I've worked very hard in my life and in many ways I've achieved great success. I can provide for your mother, sister, and you in ways most of my countrymen can only dream of."

"Yes, I know, but..."

"I can ensure we have a beautiful home, the best carriages, and the finest clothes. My success has allowed me to hire the best governesses for you and Cecile, and you've received the finest education money can buy. Do you realize there are many young men who can't say they've received the education you girls have?"

"Yes, Father. But I..."

"But there are things that will always be out of my reach, no matter how wealthy or successful I am. I want to see you and your sister securely married. Cecile I worry less about, but you're twenty-five now, and your choices are fewer. I don't agree with that, but this is the way of the world."

Annelisa saw there was no point in interrupting her father again. He needed to explain his reasons for wanting her to tolerate a life without love married to a man who couldn't even be bothered to feign kindness toward her in front of her own father. What she needed to say would have to wait.

"I know the Earl of Swindon is a bit mature, but he can give you something—give this family something—I never can. You will be Lady Annelisa Sutcliffe. You may not see the importance of this now, but when the earl's titles pass to your sons, you will see how my choices today made life better for this family for generations to come."

The thought of doing what she'd done with Nikolai with Thornton Sutcliffe made her stomach turn. She could only imagine how terrible it would be to have that callous oaf on top of her as she closed her eyes to block out the sight of his old face and body. There would be no French, no gentle kissing of her neck, no gazing into pale blue eyes the color of the sky.

"I understand some of this is my fault, Annelisa. I've spoiled both you girls, but you even more. Maybe if I hadn't been so successful you'd understand the value of what a marriage to a man like the earl offers."

Annelisa felt any guilt she'd had about what she'd tell her father quickly evaporate now. So she had no right to expect love or respect from the man she'd marry and because she did expect these things she was spoiled? She knew exactly what the value of her marriage to the Earl of Swindon was. He would receive a great deal of her father's money to stave off his near bankruptcy, and her father would gain from the earl what he'd never been able to obtain on his own—a much higher social position.

That she'd gain nothing and lose everything she held dear meant nothing to either of them, it appeared.

"So I'm very pleased to see your mood has improved from last night, my dear. What did you want to discuss with me?"

Annelisa forgot about everything she'd practiced that morning to say to her father. The words "spoiled" and "value" rang in her ears, infuriating her.

"Well, Father, I am in a much better mood today, but not because I've accepted marriage to Thornton Sutcliffe. I still have no interest in marrying some old man who shows no interest in my current or future happiness. I don't care if he's an earl, or a duke, or Queen Victoria's brother! I don't want to marry anyone, but especially the wretched Earl of Swindon. And if I do ever marry someone, it will be because I love him and he loves me."

Andrew Fielding grimaced as he sat back in his chair. "I had hoped you'd had a change of heart when I saw your smiling face in the doorway, but I see now that is not the case. Well, nothing has changed. You'll still marry the earl in a month's time, so you'd better get used to it."

Annelisa rose to her feet and steadied herself with her hands on the desk. Adrenaline pumped through her body as she prepared to announce her news.

"Everything has changed, Father. I will not be marrying the earl because I no longer possess the one thing of value he seems to believe I, or any other woman, should own."

"What do you mean?" her father said nervously.

"Thornton Sutcliffe wants two things from this family: your money and my virginity. As of last night, only one of those things is available to him."

Her father sat in his chair dumbfounded. Her words hung in the air like the heavy smoke that poured from the Fielding factories' smokestacks, and just like the smoke, they cast a pall over everything.

Annelisa waited for him to reply, to say anything, but he simply stared up at her as if she were a stranger. She steeled herself for his eventual reaction, which she was sure would be full of pure rage.

His first movement was to stand and just as she had, he braced himself with his hands on the desk. The effect was one of two adversaries facing off against one another. For a long time they stood like that until he finally spoke, his voice full more of concern than anger.

"How could you do this? Do you realize what you've done?"

"I know exactly what I did. I saved myself from being trapped in a loveless marriage that benefited everyone but me."

"You don't know the half of it, Annelisa. I will have to pay the earl to keep him from disgracing you. If I don't, he'll let everyone know what you've done."

"Is that all that matters to you? Does my happiness mean nothing to you?"

The tears began to well up in her eyes, and Annelisa stepped away from the desk, shaken by her father's words. His silence gave her his answer and his stony stare showed her how little he thought of her happiness.

"Jane!" he bellowed for the maid.

A young woman in a telltale black and white maid's uniform appeared almost instantly, a look of terror on her face. "Yes, Mr. Fielding."

"Where's Mrs. Fielding?"

"In the garden, sir."

"Tell her I need her here now."

The maid skittered away to find Annelisa's mother, leaving her alone with her father once again.

"I want you to tell your mother what you told me. Watch how she takes your news."

"I will tell whomever you'd like that I willingly did what I had to do to save myself from what you would force me to do."

"I always knew you were willful..." Andrew Fielding broke off his sentence and stormed over to join his wife in the doorway.

"Eleanor, close the door. Annelisa has something she needs to tell you. Go ahead. Tell her."

In a far less combative tone, she said to her mother, "I won't be marrying the Earl of Swindon because I am no longer a virgin, which was part of the deal to marry me."

Annelisa saw the blood drain from her mother's face and then Eleanor Fielding staggered toward a chair, as if her words had sapped all her mother's strength. Her father moved to support her and remained standing behind her.

"Why would you do this?" her mother asked in a sad voice.

Could her mother ever understand even if she explained her reasons? She'd always seemed confused by her daughter's behavior, often calling her "modern" as if the description were an insult. Would she relate to the idea of wanting to be more to a man than a breeder?

Before she could begin to explain, her father spoke up. "I don't care why anymore. What I want to know is who the man is. He will do right by her and marry her, or I'll see him shot. Tell me his name."

"I will not reveal his name, Father."

Shock registered on Andrew Fielding's face. "Why? Is he not an honorable gentleman who would do the right thing?"

"He is very honorable, but I don't want to marry

him or anyone else. I will not be forced into marriage, regardless of the man."

Annelisa stormed out of her father's study, leaving her stunned parents to figure out her meaning. Locking herself in her room, she congratulated herself for standing up to her father's antiquated attitude. Now all she could do was pray she wasn't pregnant with Nikolai's child.

Four

Nikolai settled in to his bed after a long day of negotiating diplomatic efforts. Often his days were filled with events that appeared more social than work, but the past few days had been some of the most taxing since his arrival in Britain. With events in Eastern Europe continually changing, mostly for the worst, and the new German state disrupting the whole of Europe since its birth just seven years earlier, he saw more work and less drinking with the English in his future.

As he let his muscles relax, he thought about his rendezvous with Violet in the Stewarts' garden. Never before had he been so careless. As a diplomat, he was expected to behave with the utmost discretion, and as a rule, he did. Normally, the thought of fucking a strange woman at a ball just yards from hundreds of party guests would be dismissed in disgust as something far too dangerous.

But something about Violet Moceanu had made him disregard everything he held dear.

He raised her glove to his nose to inhale the scent of her perfume that lingered on the fabric. Its spicy sweetness seemed so familiar, yet he continued to draw a blank as to where he'd smelled it before and on whom. He'd recognized it as soon as they'd begun speaking, its unique fragrance softly wafting up from Violet's neck and wrists to his nostrils. The perfume had been intoxicating later as he'd nuzzled near her ear.

The memory of their time together thrilled him even now days later, and as he lay in bed replaying the events of that night, his cock began to harden. She'd been so tight when he'd entered her, he'd wondered if she was a virgin. He dispelled that thought almost as quickly as it came, however. Virgins didn't seduce men as Violet had him.

He'd wanted her the moment they began talking in the garden. Rarely had he been so fortunate as to meet such an intelligent woman. Most women seemed content to be told things—what to say, how to act, how to dress—but it was a rare woman who possessed a mind of her own. He admired a woman who could think for herself.

They'd had a genuine conversation with both of them contributing. How long had it been since he'd gotten to enjoy that? When she'd touched his arm, a clear signal she desired more than just stimulating conversation with him, he'd felt a twinge of disappointment. How refreshing it had been to enjoy another's company simply through the exchange of ideas!

Not that the opportunity to make love to her had been a disappointment or something he dreaded. Even without seeing her entire face because of the mask, he'd found her stunning. Blessed with a body that would please any man, she captivated him physically with little more than a touch.

Rarely before had he been so attracted to a woman, not to mention one he'd just met. It seemed unlikely he would see her again, however. Something had happened to make her flee from their coupling, but he couldn't place what it could be still days later.

Dozens of possibilities ran through his mind, threatening to tarnish his memories. There was no point in recriminations now. Whatever it had been, it was over. All he had was her glove and the memory of an enchanting woman who'd given him a night of pure pleasure. Anything else he wished it could be was just that—a wish.

The Fielding household appeared to be in a state of excitement, and Nikolai doubted his arrival was the cause. As he waited in the hallway for Andrew to finish his meeting, he sensed the household staff nearby whispering and tittering about something.

The door of the study opened and out marched the Earl of Swindon, Andrew's soon-to-be son-in-law. Nikolai had to step out of his way to avoid getting run over as the earl left, slamming the door behind him.

"Nikolai, please join me," Andrew said as he turned back into his study.

As he made his way toward the door, bits and pieces of a conversation reached Nikolai's ears.

"She's lost yet another one. That girl loses them more often than anyone I've ever met."

"You better tell her mother, but I'd wait. The poor lady has had a difficult week."

Confused but curious if this had something to do with the furious exit of the earl, Nikolai entered Andrew's study and sat beside him in front of the fireplace. The pained look on his friend's face told him something serious had occurred since he'd last visited three days ago.

"I'm afraid I'm not prepared for our meeting today, my friend. Please don't think this is any reflection on your interests. I'm still as much a supporter of enhanced British-Russian relations as I've ever been, and I hope I can still count on your support for my business interests in your country."

"Of course. If you'd prefer, we can reschedule."

Andrew Fielding looked up toward the ceiling. "Yes, yes. We can certainly reschedule. It's been a very trying day."

"Andrew, may I help with anything?"

After a deep sigh, he replied, "I wish you could."

Nikolai remained silent as his friend sat pinching the bridge of his nose, his eyes closed. More than once, he sighed and looked up. Nikolai thought he might speak, but then he simply returned to pinching his nose again.

While he waited, Nikolai's mind wandered back to the masquerade ball and Violet.

He slid his hand into his coat pocket and fingered her glove. As foolish as he knew it was, he enjoyed the idea that part of her still remained with him. His fingers toyed with the soft fabric as he remembered her soft lips on his, almost unsure in their exploration of him.

She'd been bold yet tentative in her seduction, a strange contradiction that wouldn't leave his memory. Would he see her again? The idea brought a smile to his face and for a moment, he enjoyed the fantasy.

"The marriage has been called off."

Nikolai was yanked out of his daydream back into the present by his friend's somber announcement. "Pardon?"

"My daughter won't be marrying the Earl of Swindon at the end of the month."

That explained Sutcliffe's leaving earlier, but Nikolai felt no regret for Andrew's dashed hopes. The earl's boorish behavior was nothing Annelisa Fielding should be forced to tolerate. But it was obvious that his friend was disappointed.

"I'm sorry your plans haven't worked out, Andrew."

"And she's going to be ruined if I don't pay him the money I promised would accompany the marriage."

Nikolai's hands balled into fists. That villain Sutcliffe was just the type to use some slight or tiny imperfection in her to take her father for all he could.

"Thornton Sutcliffe is a cad. Be happy he's shown his colors now before you presented him one of your children."

Andrew hung his head and in a defeated voice said, "It wasn't the earl who misused Annelisa. She misused him...and me."

"My friend, whatever that sorry excuse for a man claims she did is a lie. I simply cannot believe your lovely daughter could misuse anyone."

Never looking up, Andrew explained, "She allowed a man to take her maidenhead just nights ago knowing the earl sought a virgin for his bride. And now she refuses to identify the man who deflowered her. The earl doesn't know, but he has to assume that this can be the only reason I'd withdraw my approval of the marriage. If he talks, she'll be ruined."

Nikolai sat stunned by Andrew's words. Was it possible?

"Are you sure? When did it happen?"

"The night of the Stewarts' masquerade. She deceived her mother and me and snuck off while we were away."

Sure his friend could see the guilty expression written all over his face, Nikolai turned away to face the window. The room seemed to shrink and close in on him, and his chest tightened as his breath caught in his lungs.

He'd made love to Annelisa Fielding. And he'd taken her virginity. He was the man guilty of ruining Andrew's dreams.

Nikolai's stomach turned, and he struggled for air. It was his duty, as a gentleman and Andrew Fielding's friend, to confess what he'd done and make every effort to right the situation. While he fought to keep his composure, he watched as his mystery woman strolled in the garden just outside the window.

Had she harbored feelings for him or was their time together part of a plan to rid herself of the loathsome earl? Nikolai's mind leapt from one possibility to the next, settling on nothing definitive. But one thing he knew for sure.

He had to find a way to be alone with Annelisa and soon.

Turning back to face her father, he asked, "Do you believe she will relent and give up the man's name?"

Andrew shook his head. "I doubt it. My guess is that the man meant little to her. She simply wanted to ensure she wouldn't have to marry the earl."

His friend's words stung, and the last of Nikolai's fantasy about Violet—Annelisa—disappeared. He had to speak to her!

Jumping to his feet, he abruptly announced, "I must go, Andrew. We'll continue this another time, I promise."

His head hung, Andrew said, "Of course. I understand."

Nikolai knew that his friend believed he was passing judgment on him and he regretted that, but he'd make it up to him later. Now, he had to find Annelisa.

With a quick pat on his friend's shoulder, Nikolai left hoping to find her still in the garden. Impulsively, he charged out the front door and made his way toward where he'd seen her, never considering she may not be alone.

He spied her near the gazebo at the far end of the garden. She appeared to be upset—or was it sadness her face conveyed? No matter. He would make things right and from this day forward strive to ensure all her days were happy ones.

"Miss Fielding?"

Annelisa turned slowly toward him and smiled. "Yes, Count Shetkolov?"

Nikolai approached her cautiously as to not frighten her. When he reached her, he whispered, "I think it may be permissible for us to use our first names considering our recent history."

The smile disappeared from her face, replaced by a look of surprise. Her voice, however, betrayed nothing more than its usual politeness.

"Recent history, sir?"

"There's no need for any more lies, Annelisa. I know it was you at the ball. And I intend on doing the honorable thing, I assure you."

"The honorable thing?"

"Why, of course. I'll confess to your father my part in our rendezvous and properly ask for your hand in marriage. While what we feel may not be love now, I believe it will grow in time and we can be quite happy."

Bending down on one knee, Nikolai took her hand in his and gazed up into her eyes. "I pledge to make you happy and take care of you, as I know you will me."

While he'd never proposed marriage before, he was sure her stunned reaction wasn't common. But perhaps she'd underestimated his honor.

"Did you think I'd abandon you when you need me most?"

"Count Shetkolov, please get up."

Nikolai rose and stared down at her, liking what he saw.

"Sir, please forgive me, but I no more want to marry you than the Earl of Swindon. While I'm positive you are an honorable man, I simply don't want to marry anyone at all."

Nikolai stood stunned. "Pardon?"

"I see by your expression that I've offended you. I am sorry. But I'm not in need of a husband."

"But what we did in the Stewarts' garden..."

"Was what I had to do to be free of the earl. Nothing more, Count."

"Please call me Nikolai. And it was far more than what you say. I took your virginity, and for that we must marry. I would be a scoundrel if I allowed you to face this alone."

Annelisa smiled and touched his hand. "Nikolai, for that I must thank you for you helped me retain my freedom. I am sorry I had to resort to tricking you, but if I remember correctly, you enjoyed yourself. Let's leave it at that—an enjoyable experience each of us will remember."

Nikolai glared down into the face of this obstinate woman.

"Uprymaya!"

"What does that mean?"

"Perhaps French would be better, mademoiselle. Fille tetue."

Annelisa dropped his hand and stepped back.

"Stubborn girl?"

"Yes, and if you won't agree to marriage, I'm sure your father will when I confess to him that I'm the man he seeks."

"You wouldn't! He'd be furious. He'd never forgive you."

"Oh, I'm sure he'd be angry, but he likes me. In time, he'd forgive me."

Nikolai held out his hand and waited for Annelisa to take it. "Shall we?"

All confidence drained from her face. "Don't do this, please! You don't love me, and I don't love you. Why would you want to marry me?"

"Because it's the right thing to do."

"Why is everyone always telling me what they want to do is the right thing?"

Ignoring her question, he repeated his question and added, "Or perhaps you'd prefer I approach him myself?"

Nikolai began to walk back toward the house. In truth, his stomach was in knots over telling her father what he'd done, but he had to show her he meant business. If she even thought he might be anything less than strong now, she'd never respect him as a husband.

Annelisa ran in front of him and stopped him with her hands on his chest. "Please, Nikolai! Don't do this. I'll do anything you require. Just not marriage."

Every word from her mouth insulted. Did she believe him to be unworthy of her hand?

"Anything I require?"

"Anything!"

So now she was willing to submit to anything he required as long as it wasn't marriage to him? What about everything? That would be better yet.

"Then anything it shall be, Annelisa. The cost of your freedom will be the continuation of what we began at the Stewarts' ball. Unless you're willing to do this, I will leave to speak to your father now."

"The continuation of..." she stammered.

Nikolai watched as her face grew red. "There's no reason to be bashful now, Miss Fielding."

"So I am to be your sex slave?"

Finally, something had left her mouth that didn't offend him. "Sex slave? No, not exactly. I'm looking forward to your efforts showing the eagerness of our first time together."

"I thought you were an honorable man, Count Shetkolov."

Nikolai chuckled at her attempt to sway him through his honor. "I'm not the one who began this, my dear, but I see nothing dishonorable in what we are to do."

Annelisa stood looking up at him, a look of exasperation on her face. Nikolai enjoyed her irritation and hoped his words had bothered her as much as hers had him.

"You leave me with no choice then. Either I am to be your unwilling wife or your willing concubine, but I must be one."

Ordinarily, he would agree with her assessment of his behavior as lacking honor, but the combination of wanting her again and wishing to retaliate for her insults blinded him to the impropriety of his demands. At the moment, though, the pleasure of watching her chafe under his power over her was perfect.

"I will expect you at my home tomorrow at three."

"And if I refuse?"

"Then we speak to your father and at the end of the month, we will be married."

Annelisa turned on her heels and stormed away ahead of him before spinning back toward him, as if she'd suddenly remembered something important.

"Is it true you are soon to be recalled to St. Petersburg?"

Grinning, Nikolai took his time answering as he walked toward her. When he stood in front of her, he leaned down to inhale her sweet perfume and whisper in her ear, "You won't get rid of me that easily, my dear Annelisa."

Nikolai's home loomed at the end of a long stone pathway that connected the house to the road. Annelisa stood hesitant to take that final step toward what would happen that afternoon. Was she truly going to go through with it? Was she going to make love with Nikolai Shetkolov? Was there no way out of the arrangement?

She tried to convince herself that this would be no different than what they'd done at the masquerade ball, but to no avail. This would be nothing like that. Then she'd had a mask and had acted like a worldly French woman. Now she'd be laid bare, seen by him, and her inexperience would be obvious.

Cursing her foolishness for ever thinking her plan would be successful, she furtively looked around to ensure no one saw her and stepped onto the first stone on the path to his front door.

If this is what I must do to keep my freedom, then this is what I'll do. At least he's not the Earl of Swindon.

Each step was accompanied by an increase of butterflies in her stomach. In minutes, he'd know she had only the knowledge of books when it came to lovemaking.

Annelisa mumbled to herself, "Oh, what does it matter? If he doesn't like me, perhaps he'll free me from this deal with the Devil. If not, then I only have to withstand this until he's called home, unless I can devise a way out."

Her pep talk buoyed her spirits, and with a deep breath, she stepped onto his front porch and knocked at the door. She was surprised when he answered only in his shirt and trousers.

"Come in."

As she walked over the threshold, she knew there could be no turning back. Once inside the entrance hall, she quickly looked around for any signs of the household staff but saw none.

"Where is your help?"

Nikolai closed the door and walked past her into the parlor. "There's only a manservant who attends me, the maid, and a cook. I gave them the afternoon off so there could be no chance of gossip. No one knows you're here, unless you told them."

"No, I told no one."

She hadn't even told Cecile, mainly because there would be no way she'd keep this secret. Plus, her sister had already taken a liking to him, so she'd never understand why she wouldn't love to be his wife. But worst of all, if Cecile knew she was here and the reason why, she'd know her plan had failed.

No, it was better no one knew what she was about to do.

Nikolai had already sat down on the settee, and Annelisa looked around the room for somewhere else to sit other than next to him, but there was no other piece of furniture available. Not a chair. Not even a stool!

"What kind of house has only one place for guests to sit down? Where is the rest of your furniture?"

As Annelisa faced him, she saw that he was enjoying her discomfort. He sat with his legs opened, his head leaning against the back of the settee, and slyly grinned at her.

"I removed them."

"You removed them? What on Earth for?"

"I didn't see any reason to give you the chance to drag this out. So come sit down next to me and we can at least talk a bit."

Annelisa couldn't contain her nervousness and fear, and before she knew it, evidence of them both came out for Nikolai to see.

"Why are you doing this? Have I offended you in the past and this is my payback?"

Never letting the grin leave his face, he answered, "I haven't done anything yet, and other than your refusal to marry me, I don't think we've ever had a full conversation before yesterday...well, not counting the night at the ball. So, no, you aren't being paid back for any offense."

Annelisa turned away to conceal the tears that began

to well up in her eyes from her frustration. There was no way out of this.

"Come, sit with me."

When she didn't move, he said in a softer voice, "Annelisa, please come sit next to me. I enjoyed our talk the other night and hoped we could continue it here before we do anything else."

Resigned to her fate, she turned around slowly to see the taunting grin gone and a look of genuine happiness on his face. Cecile's comment about his eyes flashed through her mind as she looked into them. There was something beautiful about their pale blue color next to his sandy colored hair.

As she sat down on the sofa, careful to keep as much distance between them as possible, she avoided looking at him. "What would you like to talk about? I enjoyed our discussion of Italian gardens."

"While I enjoyed that myself, I'd like some answers first."

Nikolai took her chin between his thumb and forefinger and gently turned her face toward him. "Look at me, Annelisa. I'd like some answers."

She closed her eyes, afraid of what he'd ask. He seemed so close...too close.

"Did you pick me simply because you thought I'd never figure out who you really were?"

Annelisa's eyes flew open and she swore she saw an expression of hurt on his face.

"No, it wasn't like that at all."

"Then why me?"

Looking down at her hands in her lap, she said quietly, "Because you're honorable and respectable. And I wouldn't choose anyone in my social circle."

She didn't have the heart to add that she'd heard he'd be soon returning to Russia.

"Your actions were rash. What if you're with child now?"

"I know. I remembered too late that I hadn't taken any precautions."

"You understand if you are, you'll have no choice but to marry me. I won't allow my child to be a bastard."

"Oh, I've made such a mess of things! All I wanted was to ensure I didn't have to marry the Earl of Swindon. Now I may be pregnant and forced to marry anyway."

Nikolai remained silent, and Annelisa feared she'd insulted him. "I'm sorry. I didn't mean to offend you."

"Why are you so against marriage? Or is it just to me or Thornton Sutcliffe?"

This was a topic she was passionate about, and she rose to her feet as she answered. "I'm against the idea that I, or any woman, should be traded like cattle to simply improve a man's life. I never wanted to be Lady anyone, but my father wants that for me, so my marriage was arranged. I never loved the earl, but he needs my father's money, so my marriage was set. But what about me? What about what I want and need?"

Before she realized it, she'd paced back and forth in front of him lecturing on her ideas of marriage. When she was finished, she saw him grinning up at her again.

"What's so funny?"

"Nothing's funny. However, I definitely know your mind on marriage now."

Annelisa returned to the settee and turned toward him. "I'm sorry. That was a bit much. It's not that I have any inherent problem with marriage. I just believe I should be more involved in who I marry and why. Do you know there are some who believe just as I do? They also believe women should get the right to vote and some measure of equality with men."

"I had no idea Andrew Fielding's daughter was such a radical."

"Is it radical to believe women are capable human beings? Is it radical to believe marriage should be based on love instead of money or status or worst of all, convenience?"

Shaking his head, Nikolai smiled. "No."

Annelisa sat quietly as the butterflies returned to her stomach. Their discussion of marriage had ended, and as he sat silently next to her, she was sure the reason for her visit would begin at any moment.

Nikolai liked the fiery look she got in her eyes when she talked about subjects she was passionate about. Even though he was sure she was frightened of what was to come, he saw a strength in her she may not even have known existed.

Bringing her hand to his lips, he softly kissed it. "No more talk of marriage. Agreed?"

Annelisa nodded. "Then what should we speak of?"

"No more talking," he whispered as he leaned in and placed a single soft kiss just below her ear.

The scent of her perfume—that fragrance that had haunted him—drifted into his nose, enchanting him. So delicate yet so desirable.

"Nikolai, I..."

Annelisa's voice trailed off as he continued to caress the tender skin of her neck with his lips. When he moved up to her mouth, he took her face in his hands.

"Annelisa, there's no reason to be afraid. We know each other this way already. Let yourself enjoy this, and let me give you what you gave me."

Before she could answer, he covered her mouth with his and slipped his hand behind her head, pulling her to him. Her mouth opened under his, and he slid his tongue over hers. Slowly, he flicked the tip over her lips and back into her mouth.

Despite her actions at the ball and what he'd believed, he sensed her inexperience now. The confident and seductive Violet was gone, but in her place he found a woman whose near innocence charmed him. As he kissed her, more and more he found himself falling for her.

"Nikolai...I..."

"What's wrong?"

Annelisa hesitated. "The first time we were together...I was...I mean..."

Nikolai kissed her on the lips. "I know. I suspected that night, but I know."

"No, I don't mean about being a virgin. I mean it was different. I had a mask on. I didn't feel so...so exposed."

Annelisa looked away, but he pulled her back to meet his gaze. "This shouldn't be something you fear. Pleasure should make you happy. I promise you'll like it."

Trailing kisses up her neck, he heard her say quietly, "I guess I don't have much choice, do I?"

Nikolai didn't answer her and returned to kissing her neck. He didn't like blackmailing her. When he'd first demanded she continue what they'd begun at the ball, it had been a reaction to her rebuff. It hadn't taken long for that to wear off, leaving a desire for her in its place. He'd rather her come to him willingly, but if he couldn't have that, he'd take this.

Never had a woman had such an effect on him! Whether as the seductress Violet or the innocent Annelisa, she made his body come alive like never before. Just kissing her made his cock stiffen, and in no time he was wishing to be inside her like just nights before.

But today wasn't about him. Today was the first step in her desiring him.

Gently, he lowered her onto her back and positioned himself over her. How beautiful she looked as she stared up at him!

When he began inching his hand up her leg, she flinched and he waited for her rejection, but none came. Never taking his eyes from hers, he watched excitedly for her response as his hand caressed her thigh. He wasn't disappointed.

As his hand slowly slid to her inner thigh, Annelisa closed her eyes and sighed. But would she allow him to reach his goal?

Carefully, he eased his hand toward the V between her legs. Her dress concealed what he'd soon touch, but as his fingertips first grazed her downy hair, he instantly knew she hadn't closed her eyes in fear.

With one finger, he stroked between her damp curls, feeling her soft folds as he watched her expression change to pure desire. Opening her eyes, she looked up at him with a pleading look. Over and over, his fingertip slid through her moisture, grazing her excited clitoris.

It would be so easy to bury himself in her. She was wet and willing. Putting these ideas out of his mind, he eased back his hand to pull up her dress.

"Nikolai?"

He heard how unsure she was as her voice broke and wanted to reassure her. Dipping down, he kissed her lips and stroked her cheek.

"Trust me."

Raising her dress, he piled it above her waist and slid down to see what his lips and tongue eagerly desired. Within her glistening brown fleece sat a swollen, pink nub begging for his mouth's attention.

Licking his lips, he whispered, "Yes," just as he touched it. Gently at first, he planted soft kisses on her, as she whimpered above him.

As his mouth began to pleasure her, he slid a finger down her slick seam and carefully entered her. She was so tight around his finger!

"Oh, Nikolai! I...it feels so..."

Spurred on by her words, he worked to bring her to orgasm. Every drag of his tongue over her cunt sent pleasure through her and with every sensation, she moaned and pleaded for him to continue.

She tasted so good on his tongue, and he greedily lapped her, wanting more. Musky sweet, her flavor excited him. Slowly, he became conscious of her leg pushing against his cock—no rubbing, like she was trying to pleasure him.

The feeling was exquisite. Every touch of her leg on his swollen cock brought him closer to coming. As his body careened toward its own release, his mouth sensually devoured her cunt and his finger fucked her.

Sure he would come before she did, he maneuvered his body away from her leg, instantly missing the feel of her on him. But he wanted her to have today what she'd given him.

She buried her hands in his hair, pulling him tightly to her and he knew she was close. A few more licks and thrusts and she'd come apart. Taking her clit in his mouth, he sucked her just to the point of no return and when her body clenched around his finger, he gently began nibbling her swollen nub, sending her over the edge.

"Oh, God! Please don't stop. Don't ever stop!"

Her body shook under his touch, and he rode her orgasm until all that was left were minor shocks and quivering that continued to wrack her spent body. Eager to see her face, he rose to his knees but saw nothing he expected.

Why was she crying? He knew she'd enjoyed everything he'd done, so why the crying?

"Annelisa, what's wrong?"

She scrambled to cover herself as she sat up, tears beginning to stream down her face. "Nothing. Nothing's wrong."

Nikolai sat back unsure of what to do. His plan had backfired, and it was only their first time together. Where had the strong, fiery woman from earlier gone to?

Annelisa jumped to her feet. "I have to go. Please don't tell my father about the ball. I know I have to abide by our agreement, but I really must go."

Before he could answer and console her about whatever was upsetting her, she ran out the door. At the window, he watched as she ran to the road and stopped.

Had she had a change of heart?

As he waited to see if he should go to her, Annelisa suddenly swayed and crumpled to the ground. Nikolai bolted out the door and ran to her, finding her passed out on the side of the road. Carefully, he picked her up in his arms and carried her back into the house to one of the bedrooms.

After only a short time, she came to. "What happened? Where am I?"

"You fainted and I brought you here to ensure your safety."

"Fainted?"

Nikolai nodded and sat down on the bed next to her. "Are you feeling better?"

"I think so." Sitting up, she righted herself, smoothing her dress. "I'm fine now. Perhaps I should consult a physician. I do hope I'm not suffering from hysteria."

Nikolai grinned. "Hysteria?"

"Oh yes. And if that's the case, there's no telling how long I'd be bedridden. It could take weeks before I'm up and around again."

He took her hand in his and said, "I do hope it isn't that, my dear Annelisa, but you do know what the prescribed treatment for hysteria is, don't you?"

Her silence told him she knew exactly what he meant.

Nikolai pushed the hair from her face and leaned in toward her. "I wouldn't worry about hysteria considering our arrangement. I can assure you I plan to do everything in my power to ensure you never suffer from that particular ailment."

Six

After she agreed to return in two days, Annelisa left and Nikolai set off toward London to return to his work. As his carriage rambled along the uneven country roads toward town, he thought about Annelisa and her failed attempt at reneging on their deal.

Chuckling, he mumbled, "She's a minx, that one."

She'd almost convinced him something was wrong until she'd mentioned hysteria. With that, she'd tipped her hand. A catch-all diagnosis, hysteria was invoked by English doctors for everything from weight gain and tiredness in women to the recalcitrant wife no man knew how to handle. And fainting was a primary symptom of hysteria, as Nikolai was sure she knew.

He smiled as he thought of her beautiful face as she pretended to be sick. *She probably faked the fainting too,* he thought to himself.

He'd have to stay on his toes with Annelisa Fielding.

Her father had been right when he'd described her as intelligent. He'd also been right when he'd said she could control the world if she were a man. Rarely had Nikolai encountered a craftier politician in Britain or elsewhere he'd served who could best her wiles and cunning.

The Earl of Swindon should be thankful she did get away. She'd have taken his titles and truly left him with nothing. Would serve him right.

Nikolai stretched his legs out in front of him as the carriage continued on its way. Her tendency to manipulate didn't bother him. If anything, he enjoyed it. Nothing like a challenge to keep a man alert. And her creative way of using her intelligence meshed well with her womanly charm, which affected him considerably. In fact, it was that charm that he found far more dangerous. She had already ensnared him a bit too quickly for his taste.

The truth was he'd already fallen for her as Violet, and the change to Annelisa hadn't dampened his interest any. Closing his eyes, he licked his lips, savoring the taste of her that still lingered on them.

He preferred to remember the moments when her body had come alive under his touch—how she'd begged him to never stop tasting her, worshipping her with his lips and tongue. In those moments, she wasn't scheming her way out of marriage or their arrangement. She was just a woman who loved the pleasure he could provide.

Just thinking about the way her silky folds had felt under his tongue, the slick dampness helping it glide from her tight entrance to her quivering pink clit, made his cock strain against his pants. He looked forward to their next rendezvous, two days away.

Until then, there was the business of diplomacy to attend to.

Nikolai's carriage jerked to a halt in front of his London residence. As he stepped out onto the cobblestones, he was confronted by the troubles of the day in the person of his fellow diplomat, Maksim Androsky.

"Nikolai, where have you been? I've heard from four members of Parliament in the last hour!"

Maksim seemed even more nervous than he was by nature this night. His small stature was all-a-quiver, and his small eyes widened in excitement. Nikolai waited for him to calm down before he asked about what had obviously upset his subordinate, but his state of distress only seemed to grow with the silence.

"The British government has learned of the Treaty of San Stefano. They reject the autonomy of Bulgaria and have made it known they won't allow it."

As Nikolai headed up the steps to his front door, he attempted to allay the man's fears. "Maksim, before we move on this, let me explain something. The British government prefers to remain friends with our country. This is one treaty. Remember that."

Trailing behind him, Maksim complained, "Nikolai, I don't think you appreciate the British feeling on this treaty. The men I spoke to already want assurances that the Tsar doesn't plan on using it to expand his empire."

Maksim closed the door and hurried to catch up to Nikolai, who was already seated behind his desk composing a letter. Throwing himself into a chair, he wrung his hands while he waited for Nikolai to finish.

"Calm yourself, friend. I'm requesting a meeting with the Foreign Secretary. That will show us where the official position of this government lies."

Sitting back in his chair, he considered what he knew of the British Foreign Secretary. The Marquess of Salisbury, Robert Cecil, was by and large an unknown factor, only in the position less than a month, but Nikolai had sensed in their few meetings that he favored the Russian position in the east.

"But Nikolai, Robert Cecil may be like Prime Minister Disraeli..."

Nikolai raised his hand to stop Maksim's train of thought. The Prime Minister had been far clearer in his opinion of Tsar Alexander's actions in the recent war with the Ottomans, and Maksim's concern that the Foreign Secretary's ideas may match Disraeli's were valid. But Nikolai believed Cecil to be sympathetic to his country, so he would begin with him instead of the Prime Minister. Better to start with friends first.

"Time will tell, my friend. For now, we begin with the Foreign Secretary and go from there."

Maksim appeared to want to argue more, but Nikolai closed his eyes in what he hoped was a clear sign he didn't intend to discuss the issue further.

"How is your family, Maksim?"

Nikolai let the man talk about the various goings on of his family, thankful he could be so easily distracted. Years younger, Maksim was a novice diplomat who still had a great deal to learn about the service, but Nikolai appreciated the care he took with their assignment. He could be quite taxing when his feathers were ruffled, something he'd learn to control as he grew in the job, but in general, the young diplomat was a helpful addition to the Russian contingent in Britain.

When he'd finished providing far more personal details than Nikolai preferred to know, Maksim sat silently. Nikolai wished the two of them could remain like this—quietly in thought—but he knew him too well. A further distraction was required.

"Have you had any success in acquiring Karentin's approval for your marriage to his youngest daughter?"

Nikolai knew this would elicit a near dissertation length response from Maksim, but that was the point. He'd listened to his lamentations concerning the father of his intended as an older brother would, agreeing with his unhappiness and counseling him to remain steadfast if he truly loved the young woman. Personally, Nikolai believed it was only a matter of time before Irina Karentin's father gave his blessing to Maksim's suit, primarily due to his potential son-in-law's position in service to the Tsar.

"I am still denied, but I continue to press my case. Thankfully, I can be sure of my dear Irina's love for me. Perhaps upon my return, her father will finally agree to our marriage."

Nikolai tuned out Maksim as he explained in detail exactly what he thought of his future relative's refusal. Quickly, he slipped into the memory of his time with

Annelisa, mentally reliving each caress of her tender flesh as her body opened up to his touch.

Suddenly, what had always been enough—serving his Tsar wherever and however necessary—wasn't enough anymore. Like Maksim, he wished for the settled life of marriage, a wife, and children.

With Annelisa.

"And you, Nikolai? What fine lady will make you leave your life of bachelorhood? As a count, you must have far better opportunities than I. A countess? Or a duchess?"

"I leave the matrimonial drama up to you, Maksim," he said with a chuckle.

"Life should not be all work. Man needs a home, Nikolai. A family."

"So true, Maksim. And how do you plan to attain yours?"

Maksim sighed. "I hope to wear him down through sheer persistence. Irina believes he will say yes eventually. I must simply be patient."

A courier interrupted the men, and Nikolai rose to meet him. Handing him the letter, he instructed him, "Deliver this to the Foreign Secretary with all speed. If you are given any reply, return immediately."

"This will give us the information we need, Maksim. For now, we wait. Go home and relax. I'll contact you when Robert Cecil replies."

Nikolai patted the younger man on the back as he made his way to the door. "Enjoy a nice dinner. I'll be in touch."

Nikolai returned to his desk feeling more confident than Maksim concerning the Foreign Secretary's response. What the junior diplomat had missed because of inexperience was the subtle but important fact that Robert Cecil hadn't approached him. If he'd been truly concerned, he'd have been quick to contact Nikolai. While members of Parliament may be upset, he gauged that the situation hadn't grown to a level that was of concern yet.

Pouring himself a drink, he relaxed, letting the taste of the finest Russian vodka settle into his mouth before the liquid slid down his throat. Loosening his tie and shirt, he willed the tension of the day to drift away. Unconsciously, he stroked his goateed chin and returned to the thoughts of his journey into London.

Maksim's words upset his reverie, however. "A countess or a duchess?" These were the very real possibilities Nikolai faced in his marriage bed because of his birth. As with all Russian nobility, it was expected that he would marry in such a way as to benefit his family. What he'd want and whom he'd prefer were of no consequence.

Nikolai catalogued his potential mates in his mind, eliminating each woman as he compared her to Annelisa.

Too short. Too tall. Too old. Too uneducated. Too unappealing.

Dozens of countesses and duchesses later, he was disgusted by his personal future. Preferring not to think any more on it, he let the thought of Annelisa's face push every other thought from his mind. How beautiful she'd looked that afternoon—no, every time he'd seen her.

Devoid of an all-important title, she possessed qualities none of the nobility he'd encountered in either Russia or Britain even knew to want.

What was the outer appearance if what resided on the inside was lackluster, or worse, ugly? How many ladies, countesses, duchesses, and even princesses had he met who the world deemed worthy of admiration simply because of their physical appeal? Far too often, those same women lacked the merest hint of wit. And intelligence? It was a rare woman who possessed a level of intelligence he admired, noble or not.

But Annelisa, for all her middle class, commoner blood, had all of the traits he wished for in a woman. Her intelligence, despite her tendency to misuse it, intrigued him, and even now as he sat in the dim light of dusk drinking alone, his mind traveled back to their conversation in the Stewarts' garden.

"Does your Tsar favor this country's current moves into African regions, Count?"

Nikolai looked at the woman who walked beside him with an expression of surprise. "My lady, your interest in world affairs is remarkable, to say the least."

Violet turned her body to face him, and she tilted her face toward him almost defiantly. "Why is that, sir? Because I am a woman?"

Before he could respond, she continued. "Am I not to have a mind to think with to go along with a body to bear children with? Is a woman to be nothing more than lips to kiss, breasts to suckle, and a womb for a man's seed?"

Nikolai stood still as a statue as she spoke, stunned by her forthright language. Never had he encountered a female who exuded such strength of mind and spirit.

"What would you believe a woman to be?" he asked, more interested in her answer than he may have ever been in anyone else's.

With her masked face looking up toward his, she said, "A woman is many things, Count. She is one to love and cherish who can nourish your very soul if she's treated with respect. Just as a man can be the center of a woman's existence, so too can a woman be that for a man. But make no mistake about it, sir. Another may be central to one's happiness, but that doesn't mean happiness comes exclusively from one person."

"And what kind of man would accept this woman you describe?"

"Why, of course, the only kind of man deserving of my respect. One who is strong and confident with the desire for a true mate instead of a mere plaything at night and a glorified scullery maid the rest of the time."

Violet turned and began walking again. Nikolai hastened to catch up to her, eager to hear more of her ideas. Far more modern than he typically preferred in a woman, they were intoxicating, nonetheless. She was intoxicating, and he yearned to hear more from her.

Beside her once again, he brushed against her arm and a jolt of arousal spiked in him. He wanted her, wanted to make this strong woman cry out for him.

"You must think me excessively proud, Count," she said, teasing him as she took his arm once again.

"No, my lady. I simply wonder where such a man as you describe exists. Are French men such men?"

Squeezing his arm, she giggled. "Some, I dare say, are such men. I find Englishmen are infrequently like the men I describe. But Russian men...I'm afraid I lack the required expertise to make a judgment on them. What is your verdict on that question?"

As he explained the Russian male character, she slid her hand under his coat and slowly stroked his wrist. Her touch excited him, making his explanation trail off. When she ducked behind a hedge, he followed, wanting to feel her lips on his.

She insisted on keeping her mask, but his desire to see her lovely face was overpowered by his need for her. Her mouth met his, opening to take his tongue in, her lips sucking gently on it. Her hands skimmed down his sides and brushed over the front of his pants. The feel of her touch on his throbbing cock, even through fabric, was more erotic than he could stand.

He needed to feel her touch on him. "Use your hand on me."

Each slow drag of her hand over his cock took his breath away. Her breasts pressed against his chest still covered by a shirt, but he felt her hardened nipples pushing against her dress and scraping against him. While his left hand slid through her wet sex, he used his right hand to squeeze one excited nipple. His reward was a needy moan he wanted to hear every night for the rest of his life as he buried himself deep inside her.

"Violet..." he groaned in return before he lifted her up and slowly slid into her tight passage.

Nikolai leaned back in his chair and stretched his legs out in front of him, hoping to ease the tension his excited cock and memories of making love to Annelisa had created. Drinking the remnants of his vodka, he enjoyed the knowledge that at least he would see her soon.

Perhaps another masquerade, he thought to himself.

"Annelisa, where are you going?" Cecile called across the garden to her sister.

She'd hoped to sneak out without being noticed, but with that plan in shambles, Annelisa scrambled to concoct a believable story to explain her leaving secretly.

"To visit Mrs. Jenkins."

The oldest women in the neighborhood and disliked by most who lived near her, Mrs. Jenkins had taken a shine to Annelisa because as a child she'd never scared like the rest of the children in the neighborhood. Now as a grown woman, Annelisa was one of the few people she permitted to visit her, claiming most of her family and neighbors were "thoroughly idiotic." She had no love for Cecile either, who seemed to irritate her with her naiveté, and she made no secret of the fact that she considered her a "ninny."

"Oh." The news of her visit to the cantankerous, old Mrs. Jenkins stopped Cecile in her tracks.

"I'll be back in a few hours. Tell Mother, would you?"

"I will. But is everything all right, Annelisa?"

Was her fear of returning to Nikolai's home that clearly written on her face? Annelisa forced a smile and quickly answered, "Of course. Why do you ask?"

"You've seemed more secretive since everything that happened with the earl. Has something gone wrong with Count Shetkolov?"

Gone wrong? Like I now must continue our relationship or he'll tell Father and I'll be forced to marry him?

Annelisa leveled her gaze on her sister. "Everything is fine, Cecile. No one knows a thing, except for you, and I need to know you'll keep my secret."

"Of course I'll keep your secret! I would never betray you, Annelisa. Never!"

Taking her sister's hands in hers, Annelisa squeezed them. "Thank you, Cecile. You are my one true confidante."

Cecile looked into her eyes, her own wide with concern. "And I will forever be. You can trust me with anything. You do know that, don't you?"

"I do. Now let me be off to visit Mrs. Jenkins. You're welcome to tag along, if you'd like."

Her sister's face twisted into an expression of distaste. "No, thank you. She's never liked me as she does you."

Annelisa nodded and smiled. "I'm sure it's only because I'm more like her."

"Don't say that! You're a thousand times nicer than

that old woman."

Turning to be on her way, Annelisa waved goodbye. "Maybe you're right," she called back.

Half a mile down the road, Annelisa reached Mrs. Jenkins' home, a stately residence that seemed appropriate for a woman of her age. As she knocked on the front door, she hoped this wasn't the day the woman had chosen to leave her house. She needed her too much today.

The door opened and the old woman's butler recognized Annelisa and let her in to wait until he'd announced her. Standing in her great foyer, she prayed Mrs. Jenkins could help her while at the same time wishing she didn't need her help at all.

But Nikolai's letter had been quite clear. She was to dress in men's clothes for their rendezvous today.

Annelisa turned his demand over and over in her mind until she'd come to the conclusion that she had no clue as to why he required her to dress as a man this day or any other day, for that matter. Was this some trick to make her look foolish?

"Annelisa, what a wonderful surprise! My child, come here."

Turning toward the elderly woman, Annelisa smiled and began to make her way toward her. Short and stout, Mrs. Jenkins barely reached Annelisa's shoulders, and she bent down to hug the woman.

"Mrs. Jenkins, thank you for seeing me with no notice."

The woman looked up at Annelisa and took her hand

in hers as she made her way toward the nearby sitting room. "You know for you, dear, anytime. You're not one of those ninnies I'm related to, thank God."

She sat down on a large, well-worn chair and folded her hands on her stomach ready to discuss the world with one of the few people she genuinely liked. Annelisa took a seat on a chair that seemed as new as the day it had been made and adjusted herself to the stiffness.

"It's been too long, my dear. How are you? Please tell me I heard incorrectly and you aren't marrying some stuffed bird...what was it I heard?"

As the older woman squinted her eyes to remember, Annelisa grumbled, "The Earl of Swindon."

"Oh, yes. Oh...please tell me he's better than his father. What a dreadful man!"

"No, he's just as dreadful, but I found a way out of that, thankfully."

Reaching over, the older woman grabbed Annelisa's hand and squeezed. "That's my girl! You didn't need to be the wife of such a revolting man."

"But I've gotten myself into something else I need your help with. Do you still have any costumes from your days on the stage?" Then after a long pause, she added, "And Mr. Jenkins' days?"

Annelisa shifted uneasily in her chair. She loved Mrs. Jenkins and in some ways, she was more a maternal figure than her own mother, but somehow she couldn't imagine telling her that she needed to dress as a man because her secret Russian lover demanded it.

Seeing the confused look on her friend's face, Annelisa

moved to reassure her. "Trust me when I tell you that it isn't for anything bad."

Well, depending on whether or not you consider having a sexual rendezvous with a man who's blackmailing you bad.

Mrs. Jenkins looked intently at Annelisa's face for a long moment, as if she were studying it or looking for the truth, and then said, "Of all the people in this world, Annelisa, I trust you to be levelheaded the most. If you need something, I'm sure it's for a good cause."

Annelisa hoped she didn't look as sheepish as she felt, but she could think of no one else to turn to. Damn Nikolai! Yet another person she was forced to lie to because of him.

"What do you need?"

One deep breath and then she said the words. "I need to dress as a man."

Annelisa was sure she'd never felt more awkward in her entire life. The pregnant pause that followed her statement seemed to go on forever until she began to wonder if she'd made a mistake. But there was no turning back now.

Thankfully, Mrs. Jenkins' brain shifted into stage mode, and she began listing the various pieces of the costume needed to change a young woman into a young man.

"Trousers, yes. Shirt, yes. Hat, of course. Boots, we should be fine with."

With the basics settled in her mind, she rocked herself out of her chair and onto her feet and took Annelisa by the hand. "Come child. It's show time!"

Upstairs in a bedroom that hadn't been used in years, the old woman rifled through a trunk filled with clothes of all kinds. Gaily colored dresses unlike any Annelisa had ever seen, fine silk scarves, corsets that looked far sexier than usual undergarments—had Mrs. Jenkins worn these all those years ago? The idea of her friend as a sensual young woman made a smile creep across Annelisa's lips.

"I bet you find it hard to believe I ever wore these. Well, believe it. And someday when you're my age, you'll be able to remember when you dressed as a man. Now come down here so we can find some of Philip's clothes for you."

Methodically, the elderly woman pulled out each item of clothing from the trunk and handed it to Annelisa. In just minutes, her arms were full of everything she'd need to complete her current masquerade.

Pointing toward a dressing screen, Mrs. Jenkins said, "Go try these on and I'll look for boots and a hat."

In no time, Annelisa emerged a changed woman. Gone was her fashionable dress, replaced with a man's pants, shirt, and waistcoat, which thankfully fit quite well and seemed to hide the obvious features which pointed to her being a woman.

Standing in front of a mirror, Annelisa looked at the image staring back at her. From the neck down, she resembled any of the men in her social circle, but from the neck up...that was going to be a problem.

"Mrs. Jenkins," she said to the woman whose head was buried in a wardrobe. "What will I do about my face and hair?"

Annelisa fussed with her hair as she waited for the woman to deliver a solution. No matter what she did with it, she still looked like a female.

From inside the wardrobe, Mrs. Jenkins barked, "A wig!"

Turning toward her voice, Annelisa asked, "Do you have one?"

Her question was met by more rustling sounds and Annelisa turned back to look at her reflection. Why would Nikolai want her dressed like this? Was this all part of a plan to humiliate her? The thought stabbed at her, making her cringe. Would he do that?

Not that it would be any worse than what he'd already demanded of her. No, whatever he required she'd do if it meant keeping her freedom.

"Let's see how this looks."

Annelisa turned to see Mrs. Jenkins holding a coat and wig. She easily slid into the jacket and actually thought she looked somewhat dashing. The wig would be a different story, however. Darker than her light brown hair, it didn't seem able to hold all her hair, but with some judicious tugging and repositioning, it finally concealed the last of her truly feminine features.

Turning back to look at the finished product, she and the old woman grimaced. Even with her beautiful hair covered in a short wig and her body concealed by men's clothing, she still looked like a woman. Just a woman in men's clothes.

"Moustache!"

Spinning around, Annelisa watched as Mrs. Jenkins

returned to the stage trunk to pull out a fake moustache.

"How will this stay on my face?"

"Stage secrets. Glue that won't hurt you. Here, let's see how this looks."

Annelisa bent down to let her apply the fake hair to above her lip and cried out as she pressed it roughly to her skin.

"We need to make sure it stays on."

After a few tries, the moustache stuck and Annelisa turned to look at it in the mirror. She moved close to it until her nose almost touched its reflection and studied the area above her lip. Perhaps if another person didn't look too closely, they might just think she was a man.

"Voila!" Mrs. Jenkins exclaimed.

"Thank you so much for your help, Mrs. Jenkins."

Annelisa hugged her and hat in hand, started toward the stairs, knowing she had little time before she was expected at Nikolai's.

"Dear, before you go, remember something."

As she turned around to face the woman, Annelisa readied herself for what she feared she'd say. "Yes?"

"In the end, you have to be true to yourself."

"I will. Thank you."

Annelisa walked quickly down the road to Nikolai's house, acutely aware of the clothes that rubbed in all the wrong places. The boots Mrs. Jenkins had given her fit oddly, and every step was an effort to ensure she didn't fall flat on her face.

She was thankful no one passed her on the road as she began to think about her current situation. She hadn't been able to stop replaying their last time together as many times as she could find free moments. The feelings he'd caused in her had made her lose her composure, and as she made her way down the lane toward his home, she cringed.

Cried! Like a silly schoolgirl!

And then her ruse had failed miserably. Nikolai was no typical man, and if she intended on winning what had grown into a test of each one's intelligence, she would need more in her arsenal than a few tears, a pouty expression, and an imaginary disease.

His home came into view as she walked around a bend, and she stopped to steady herself for another of their meetings. What would he expect this time, their third time together? Nervously, she admitted to herself that the situation she found herself in was almost comical. That she worried about what he'd want her to do was silly considering that they'd already had sex once, twice if what he did their last time together was to be counted. What he'd expect would be making love in fulfillment of their agreement.

Wiping her palms on her pants, she began on her way again, chastising herself for the butterflies in her stomach. She wasn't some ninny who couldn't handle herself. She was capable and strong, and if this is what she must do to safeguard her freedom, then she would do it and without whining or simpering.

She just hoped if what she believed would occur that she could make it through without the benefit of anonymity her mask had provided her.

Each step she took toward his house was accompanied by the combination of her stomach jumping and her reassuring herself. By the time she'd reached his front door, she felt nauseous but emboldened.

An odd combination, to say the least.

She knocked once and then twice and waited. Looking left and right to ensure no one watched her visit his home, she wondered if she was early.

"Perhaps he was detained," she mumbled as her butterflies calmed themselves.

Annelisa waited for another minute and happily turned to begin her walk home. However it had happened, she'd been granted a reprieve. Suddenly, there was a spring in her step, and as she stepped down the path to the road, she took notice of the fresh smell in the air from the early spring flowers that lined the outer edges of the property.

What a lovely day, she thought as her foot touched the last stone on the pathway.

"Miss Fielding?"

The Russian accent of Nikolai's voice stopped her dead. Although she was sure it was all her imagination, it seemed as if the beautiful smell she'd just appreciated had entirely faded away and even the birds had stopped their singing.

Slowly, she turned and saw him standing in front of her with no coat on his back or hat on his head. Dressed only in a shirt and trousers, he seemed far simpler than a Russian noble and diplomat.

"Good afternoon, Count Shetkolov. I was just...I

knocked and waited but no one answered."

Nikolai nodded as if to relay his belief in her statement. "I made sure everyone was sent away for the afternoon. I was enjoying the beautiful day in the garden. Please join me."

Did she have a choice? Annelisa just hoped he wouldn't want to fulfill their bargain outdoors behind his house.

Nikolai waited for her to join him, and she took his outstretched hand to walk beside him. It felt warm and strong in hers. Earthy.

"I'm pleased you did as I asked. I knew you were a resourceful woman."

Annelisa stared at him and squinted her eyes in anger. "Was this all a ruse to make me look like a fool? Well, I hope you're happy. You got me to dress up like a man, so go ahead. Have your fun."

Nikolai stopped and turned her to face him. He took her hat off, and bent down to kiss her gently on the lips. "It was no such thing, Annelisa."

"Then did you just want to see me obey you? Was that it?"

The smile he flashed made her stomach flip, and she looked away just in case her blush was as severe as she imagined it was.

"As much as I have to admit I enjoy the idea of just once you doing as I say, it wasn't that."

Before she could ask any further, he guided her to a patch of soft grass and sat down. Annelisa nervously stared down at him, believing he intended to make love right there in the open.

"Sit. It's a lovely day. I thought we could spend our time out here."

"Out here? You want to...out here?"

Nikolai smiled as if she'd said something amusing and held out his hand again. "Sit, Annelisa."

Lowering herself to the ground, she sat on the cool grass and immediately surveyed the area around them to assess the privacy his garden afforded.

"Don't worry. The house closest to me over there is vacant most of the time. No one can see us here, no matter what we do."

If that was supposed to put her mind at ease, it didn't. If anything, his words only made her more nervous as they hinted to what he planned to do right there, in the grass, under the blue sky.

Annelisa felt like a naive schoolgirl. Hoping to calm what had blossomed into fear, she fiddled with the crease in her trousers. When Nikolai covered her hand with his, softly touching her leg, she closed her eyes and felt the sensations wash over her.

Nikolai moved his fingers back and forth across Annelisa's thigh, feeling the soft fabric of her pants under his fingertips. Her leg tensed under his hand, and he pressed lightly with his palm to calm her.

"Is it true that this government is being difficult with yours over Eastern issues?"

Damn, she had the uncanny ability to change his

focus at the worst moments. But he wasn't going to let her succeed this time.

Moving his hand up her leg, he stroked the fabric over where her thigh met her body. Her trembling told him now she would be the one who would struggle to remain focused.

"No, not at all. Your information is faulty, dear lady."

"Oh."

Nikolai inwardly smiled at the fact that he'd been able to distract her this time, if the flutter in her voice was any indication. He continued to drift his fingers over the crease of her thigh, pausing each time near her hip.

"So what have you done since I last saw you?"

Annelisa appeared to wrestle with her thoughts. "I...I...read a book. A wonderful book. On land and its economic value."

Unable to stop a laugh from escaping, he chuckled and said, "You are an interesting woman, Annelisa. While other women spend their time gossiping and scheming for husbands, you're reading books on economics."

"Why is that funny?"

Nikolai's hand drifted onto her lap. "It's not. But not everything worth knowing can be found in books."

He pressed his hand gently against her sex and watched her eyes grow wide. "I know of no book to teach you about this."

Flustered, she answered, "That's not true. I've read everything I can on the subject, so there is knowledge to be gleaned on it."

"What subject?" he asked, toying with her verbally

and physically.

"What?"

"What subject are you referring to?"

"What men and women do..."

Smiling, he turned her face toward him. "Making love. Or fucking, if you prefer."

Annelisa's cheeks turned a bright red and she averted her gaze from his. Nikolai couldn't decide which version of the woman he liked best: the confident seductress, which he knew was merely an act, the headstrong, intelligent young woman he and others saw in public, or this far more innocent woman who blushed at his raw language.

"There's no need for embarrassment."

Her eyes darted back to meet his. "I'm not embarrassed. But I don't see the need to play with me. That is what you're doing, isn't it?"

Nikolai unbuttoned the top buttons of her shirt and slid his hand in to caress the tops of her breasts. Leaning in toward her, he whispered, "I haven't begun to play, Annelisa."

Dipping his head, he planted soft kisses on the swell of her breasts, one then the other, feeling them grow warm at his touch.

"Why are you teasing me like this?" she asked, her voice sounding strangled.

Nikolai lifted his head and looked up at her. "No teasing. If I were teasing, I wouldn't be planning to be inside you in mere minutes."

The look on her face confused him. Was that fear or

desire he saw in it?

He ran his hands down her sides, happy to see her costume was authentic and there was no evidence of a corset. He wouldn't expect to find one, even if she'd worn a dress. He'd noticed that, ever the iconoclast, Annelisa preferred the artistic style over the restrictive, but more popular, corseted dress with its bustle.

With little effort, she could be out of her men's clothes and naked under him right there in the garden. A first for him, he was sure it would be an exceptional experience.

"But what if someone is watching, Nikolai?"

The fear in her voice registered on his heart. He had made sure their privacy was assured, but if she was truly afraid, he saw no need to torment her.

Lifting his face to hers, he kissed her mouth tenderly and stroked her cheek. "Your plea touches me, love. To make you happy, we'll leave nature to its own devices and go inside."

Annelisa nodded. "Thank you, Nikolai. I can only imagine what would happen to your reputation if we were found."

Smiling, he rose to his feet and took her hand to help her up. "I can't imagine making love to one's wife would be offensive to anyone in my circles."

She stopped dead and stared at him. "We are not married, Count Shetkolov. This arrangement allows me to keep my freedom, no more. In fact, other than cementing in my mind the opinion that you're a rogue, I can't figure out what benefit this bargain of ours gives you."

In a rush, Nikolai pulled her tightly to him and kissed

her passionately. When he was done, he lifted her chin and looked directly into her eyes. "We will be married if someone finds out about our meetings. And as for what I get, don't spend another moment on it. Just know our arrangement suits me just fine."

The stunned look on her face also suited him, and before she could answer, he whisked her into the house and closed the door behind them. There was a time for the verbal sparring she so excelled at, but now was not it. Now he wanted what he'd waited for since that night at the masquerade ball.

"I want you out of those clothes. This time I get to see every inch of you."

Nikolai didn't bother to wait for a response before he resumed kissing her. While his lips tended to hers, his hands tugged at her coat, waistcoat, and shirt before moving to her trousers. As each article of clothing fell to the floor, he moved to the next until she was left standing in her drawers and looking unbelievably charming. He made quick work of those, however, and in seconds she was close to as God intended.

She was breathtaking!

As he began stripping the layers of clothing from his body, he ordered, "Take your shoes and stockings off."

Annelisa slipped out of them and turned back to face him. "I'll have no choice but to marry you if someone happens upon us. All this clothing will be impossible to get on in time to lie."

Now entirely divested of his clothes, Nikolai let his gaze roam over Annelisa's beautiful body. Full breasts sat above a small waist, which flared temptingly to sensual hips and long, gorgeous legs. All those fools who refused to see past her intelligence and stubbornness didn't know what they were missing. Such a woman—intelligent, beautiful, and built to be loved by a man—was a rare find indeed.

He intended to make her his on a far more permanent basis.

"Come here," he said in a low voice full of need. "I want you."

As he'd done minutes earlier, he roughly pulled her to him, crushing her breasts to his body. Her pebbled nipples scraped against his skin, exciting him. His mouth devoured hers, his tongue snaking between her lips to mingle with hers.

Despite her inexperience, she met his passion eagerly and wrapped her arms around his neck, pulling him even closer to her. Her slick cunt pushed against the base of his cock, driving him crazy with need.

"Moya milaya," he groaned into her mouth as he squeezed her perfect ass in his hands. He slid a finger near her wet opening and teased her, and she ground her sex against his cock wantonly.

"Nikolai...yes...yes."

"Now I begin the work to ensure you never suffer from hysteria, my love."

Lifting her in his arms, he carried her to the chaise and gently laid her down. He positioned himself over her and leaned in to kiss her lips. She arched her body up toward his and pulled his hips into hers.

Nikolai pushed his body to hers, and in a moment of perfect pleasure, buried himself in her as she moaned sweetly, "Yes."

Annelisa was conscious of little more than the desperate desire for Nikolai. When he retreated from her body, she pulled him back to her, never wanting to be without him again.

This time there was no pain, only the sublime feeling of his body joined with hers, filling it completely. Her hands pressed into his back, kneading the taut muscles that flexed and relaxed with each thrust into her as she worked to hold him to her.

He stopped for a moment and looked down at her, his pale blue eyes filled with concern. "Annelisa?"

His accent blanketed every syllable, making him seem foreign and exotic. "What's wrong?"

Desperately wishing he'd return to being deep inside her, she shook her head and pressed her fingers into the small of his back. "Please don't stop."

Nikolai plunged into her again, grazing a spot

somewhere inside her that she instantly wished he would find again. A gasp escaped her throat, and he once more stopped.

"What is it?" he asked as he searched her face.

"Nothing. I love it. Please don't stop."

Lifting his body from hers, he hovered over her, still not convinced she was all right. "I don't want to hurt you. I know you're...inexperienced."

Annelisa smiled and tugged him back to her. "Don't worry, Nikolai. I'm not hurt."

Before he could worry any more, she rolled him over onto his back and leaned down to kiss him. Whispering in his ear, she teased, "Now I'll show you my knowledge of fucking."

Sure she saw a look of surprise cross his face for just a moment, she was pleased when his hauntingly beautiful eyes looked up at her, half-lidded and clouded over by need.

Nikolai buried his hand in her hair and passionately tugged her head toward him. His lips crushed against hers as his tongue mingled with hers in a kiss unlike anything she'd ever read about in any of her books.

He was so passionate, so commanding as he moved his hands to her waist to hold her in place as he teased her wet and needy cunt with his stiff cock. She couldn't move, even if she'd wanted to, and the feel of his strong hands pushing into the flesh of her hips as he played his erotic game excited her even more.

"So you possess knowledge? Show me," he said in a voice edged with need as he slowly pushed into her.

Annelisa stiffened in surprised as he touched that spot she'd so desperately wanted him to return to. Whatever knowledge she'd believed she had seemed to fade from her mind, replaced by the singular desire to feel him touch that spot over and over.

"Yesss," she moaned as he fulfilled her silent wish with each slow thrust of his cock.

The pace of his fucking was like sweet torture. Every plunge into her was followed by a slow withdrawal as her body desperately surrounded his, not wanting to experience the loss of him. Forceful and quick was replaced by slow again and again as he controlled the pace, holding her just where he wanted her.

"Nikolai...please."

As he continued, he smiled up at her. "More?"

"Faster. God, you're driving me mad!"

Suddenly, he sat up and she was on his lap, his cock still inside her and his face just inches away. "Ride me, Annelisa."

Unsure in her mind what to do, she let her body guide her as she began sliding up and down his shaft seeking the pleasure he'd given her just moments before. But in this position she couldn't feel what she so desperately wanted. The touch of his hand as he slid a finger between her cheeks made her flinch, and she tilted her hips.

That was it! There was that feeling!

"Faster, Nikolai...right there...fuck me," she begged as he began slamming into her, hitting that perfect spot each time.

And then she was conscious of only the most exquisite

feeling traveling from deep inside her to every inch of her body as she fell on top of him. Panting, she clung to him as he continued to push into her, extending the most wonderful sensation he'd created in her.

She heard him say her name over and over in a voice that sounded like it was miles away. And then just as he had that night in the Stewarts' garden, he came inside her, flooding her body with warmth.

"Annelisa?"

Lifting her head from his neck, she looked into his eyes as her fingers played with the damp hair at his nape. "Yes?"

Nikolai leaned forward and kissed her lips softly. "It's only a matter of time before we must marry if we continue to leave things to chance."

Annelisa knew he meant no harm by what he said, but the words "must marry" rang in her ears. She didn't want to marry someone because she had to, any more than she wanted someone to marry her because they felt they had to.

But what he said was true. She couldn't continue to forget to protect herself or she'd end up as the wife of a man who had no choice but to marry her.

Climbing off him, she quickly began dressing. "Then from now on we won't rely on chance."

Out of the corner of her eye, she saw the hurt her remark had registered cross his features. His response touched her emotions, but she couldn't worry about his feelings. She didn't want a man who saw her as an obligation.

As much as she preferred to avoid him now, she had no choice but to turn and face him. She may not want to marry him, but that didn't mean being intentionally thoughtless.

He sat on the settee, still naked from their lovemaking, looking entirely too good. For a brief moment, she let her gaze travel over his face and body, and once again her body responded to him. His blond hair was disheveled after all her pulling and playing with the ends. His goatee, which she realized she'd never noticed when he kissed her, was a shade darker than the hair on his head and more closely resembled the hair between his legs. And he sat looking up at her, legs splayed open, almost looking undignified as he seemed to study her.

Suddenly uncomfortable, she pulled at her waistcoat nervously. "What?"

His blue eyes scanned her from head to toe and back again before he spoke in a deep voice that touched her somewhere no other ever had.

"Come back in two days, and make sure you're dressed like this."

A sense of rebellion surged in her. "And if I don't?"

Nikolai stretched his arms over his head and clasped his hands behind his head, leaving nothing to obscure the view of his once again excited body.

"Then we go to the church and I never have to wait for you to come back. Your choice, moya milaya."

Annelisa couldn't decide if she loved or hated the smirk he wore. As he sat there, entirely exposed to her, he seemed so unguarded, yet at the same time he exuded a power over the situation, the surroundings... her that seemed so contradictory to his current state. For a moment, she got lost in the vision of him before her.

"So which will it be, Annelisa?"

Shrinking her eyes into little slits, she glared down at him, careful to keep her gaze focused on his face instead of his raging erection. He was enjoying this!

"You know my feeling on marriage, Count Shetkolov, so you have your answer."

Smiling the grin of the victorious, Nikolai said, "I'm sure you'll understand if I don't escort you out."

"Afraid you'll offend one of your neighbors?"

He let out a laugh that even Annelisa had to admit was contagious. "You underestimate my neighbors, love."

Annelisa's mind flashed to old Mrs. Jenkins and the look on her face if she saw a completely naked Nikolai. Unable to suppress the chuckle from the thought, she said, "I think you may overestimate your appeal, Nikolai."

After changing into her dress at Mrs. Jenkins and thankful her old friend didn't seem to be too curious about her afternoon, Annelisa began the walk home. Halfway there, she realized she was still smiling and stopped short in the road.

"What am I doing? Why am I smiling? The man is blackmailing me to continue having sex with me!"

The rest of the way home she spent talking herself into disliking Nikolai. He was too old. He looked so foreign compared to every gentleman in her social circle. He was arrogant. And worst of all, he was too smart.

That flaw was the worst of his faults. Never before had she met a man who could outsmart her, yet Nikolai seemed to at every turn. Even the threat of feminine health problems couldn't dissuade him. The man was infuriating!

By the time she arrived home, she had convinced herself that he was by far the most vexing person she'd ever encountered, man or woman, and the most challenging opponent, hands down. Entering the house, however, she overheard her father in his study dealing with an actual opponent, and he was in no way like Nikolai.

"Fielding, you will amend our arrangement."

Annelisa heard her father slide his chair out from behind his desk.

"My Lord, I will do no such thing. Our arrangement was contingent upon your marriage to my daughter, and I agreed to fulfill my part to compensate you for any hardship you suffered when I withdrew my agreement to the marriage. You will get no more from me."

Her hands balled into fists as she listened to her father defend himself against the Earl of Swindon's extortion. If she were a man...

"You will and you know why. Do you want everyone else in England to know why also?"

Thornton Sutcliffe's barely veiled threat to tell everyone that she was a fallen woman struck her dumbfounded. Somehow he'd found out that she'd lost her virginity and now like the craven scoundrel he was, he was using it against her father to wrangle more money from him.

Annelisa heard her father's silence in reply to the Earl's despicable threat. Her heart broke from guilt as she waited to hear his response, knowing all too well what the next words out of his mouth would be.

"Please don't do this, my Lord. She's the apple of my eye, and your announcement would ruin her."

The Earl hissed his response. "Then I can be assured of your compliance, can't I, Fielding?"

Annelisa couldn't hear her father's usually strong voice as it dropped in defeat. Wracked with guilt for putting him in such a position, she slowly moved down the wall until she slipped into the dining room and held her hand to her mouth, sickened by the consequences of her actions.

Her poor father, forced to defend her against the likes of Thornton Sutcliffe! Regret overcame her, and she buried her face in her hands in the hopes of blocking it all out.

What a mess she'd made of everything! Both she and her father were being blackmailed, although Nikolai was nothing like the awful Earl of Swindon. But even worse, her dear father was forced to endure the humiliation of Sutcliffe's petty attacks.

Down the hallway, the door to the study opened and she heard the earl threaten, "Remember, Fielding, you have until Monday. If I don't hear from you by noon, everyone will know exactly why I chose not to marry your daughter."

Her blood boiled in anger and every cell in her body called out for justice. She fought back the urge to storm out and confront the rotten earl. She watched as he smugly walked to the front door, his dishonorable head held high as he basked in his success. Just as his hand reached the knob, he turned back and looked toward her with an expression of victory.

Turning toward her father, who stood in the doorway of the study, the earl barked, "Monday or else, Fielding!"

Andrew Fielding stood quietly as the front door slammed, his expression one of silent defeat.

Annelisa watched as her father slowly retreated into his study and closed the door. She so much wanted to go to him, but what would she say? How could she explain how sorry she was for all that she'd done?

But if she wasn't sure what to say to her father, she was perfectly clear as to what she wanted to say to the Earl of Swindon. Throwing caution to the wind, she stormed out of the house to catch up to the earl as he climbed into his carriage. She may be only a woman, but someone needed to put him in his place.

He saw her as she approached and seemed to relish the idea of the confrontation. From his perch inside the carriage, he smirked with an uncharacteristic grin, almost baiting her to give him a piece of her mind.

"My Lord, you won't get away with your blackmail. I won't let you."

Annelisa knew she was violating social conventions by speaking to a member of the peerage this way, but she didn't care. Even if he succeeded in wringing the last pound from her father, he'd know he was no better than a low life villain.

"You won't let me? Miss Fielding, you are a mere woman, and one I have on very good authority is too far beneath me to deserve any conversation with someone of my station."

Annelisa stepped back and struggled to keep her composure, feeling like she'd been slapped across the face. Something in her screamed for her to stand her ground.

"You are a cad, sir! And I am glad my father withdrew his approval for my marriage to you. You may be an earl, but to me you are a cad."

The offense of her words was written all over Thornton Sutcliffe's face, and Annelisa braced for his verbal attack. However, nothing could have prepared her for the vitriol that came from him next.

"And you are a common whore! Whatever I may have gotten for marrying you would never have been worth lowering myself to your level. You did me the greatest favor when you began your whoring, Annelisa."

Each word stung like a knifepoint digging into her skin. Before she could reply, the earl ordered his driver to leave, and Annelisa was left in a cloud of dust. Standing alone, she brushed the dirt from her hair and face and silently cursed the Earl of Swindon, wishing him nothing but a barren harpy, of the appropriate social standing, of course.

She hadn't been successful in convincing the

blackguard to end his wretched extortion, and she suspected it was just a matter of time before the entire countryside heard about her being a fallen woman. If anything, her outburst had only hastened the earl's release of his suspicions, and although she knew she should care, she didn't.

Walking back to the house, she mumbled to herself, "He deserved exactly what he got, the cad."

Annelisa locked herself in her room and lay down to forget about the whole awful event. She found herself wishing Nikolai were next to her, his arms around her as he promised in his Russian accent that everything would be fine.

How odd it was to think of him as comfort and security. She'd never looked to a man for help with any of life's troubles until recently, and now for a second time, she turned to Nikolai.

As much as she hated to admit it, he was quite charming, even for a blackmailer. And the feelings he created in her when they made love were unlike anything she'd ever experienced or even read about in her books. When he entered her, it was like the most wonderful part was being added to her.

Closing her eyes, she imagined his eyes—those stunning, pale blue eyes—and his sensual mouth, nearly hidden behind a goatee, the mouth that had introduced her body to more pleasure than she'd ever thought possible.

He definitely was very appealing.

However, something else was far more appealing.

Her freedom.

Nine

"I hope you're pleased with yourself. Some woman followed me all the way here. I thought I was going to have to outrun her."

Nikolai smiled at Annelisa, amused by the idea of a woman chasing after her. Running his hands down her back, he trailed them over her behind and gently pulled her to him. "You sound sweet."

"Why am I dressed like this again, Nikolai?"

Already excited, he pushed his cock against her and smiled. "I have a surprise for you."

"A surprise?"

He heard the concern in her voice and gently stroked her cheek. "Yes. We're going to a party."

Annelisa pushed herself away from him and stared up at him, her eyes wide with disbelief. "I'm not going anywhere. It's one thing for me to come here dressed in this costume, but I have no intention of meeting others like this."

"That's fine. I'll just speak to your father tomorrow, and we can begin planning for the ceremony."

Nikolai saw immediately the effect of his threat as she twisted her beautiful mouth into a scowl. Even dressed as a man, she looked adorable standing there completely frustrated.

"You know, that's not always going to work."

"Really? And why is that?"

Annelisa thought for a moment and by the look of irritation on her face, he saw she'd come to the same conclusion he had.

She either dealt with him this way or dealt with him as his wife. Either way, he won.

"Fine. Where are you taking me?"

Annelisa dropped herself onto the still lone piece of furniture in the parlor. Nikolai kneeled in front of her and slowly traced the seam of a pant leg up to the V between her legs. With his thumb, he drew little circles just where he knew would drive her crazy. After only a few strokes, she opened her legs more for him, her body telling him what she still refused to admit.

"Just a party with the other Russian diplomats."

Her eyes had closed with the movement of his fingers, but now they flew wide open. "Nikolai, no! They'll know I'm a woman!"

In one swift motion, he stood up and sat her on his lap facing him. Holding her by the waist, he gently pushed his erection toward her and fought back the urge to take her right there.

"Shhh. No one will know. Just don't cry out like that and no one will suspect a thing."

She dropped onto him, her head nestled in between his neck and shoulder, and mumbled, "Why are you doing this?"

In truth, he was doing this because the idea of her pretending to be someone else excited him. Just as the memory of her as a French coquette named Violet still stirred his desire, the idea of her dressing like a man made him want her even more.

"It will be fun. You'll see."

Nikolai kissed her neck softly and whispered, "We need a name for you. How does Albert sound?"

Annelisa lifted her head. "Albert?"

"Yes. It sounds perfect. Albert Fielding."

"No. Nikolai, please...someone will know."

Kissing her, he took her face in his hands. Her eyes remained closed as he said, "Annelisa, I would never let anything harm you. Trust me."

When she opened her eyes, he was sure he saw a look in them that told him she did trust him.

As much as sitting in his parlor with Annelisa on his lap pleased him, Nikolai knew it was time to go. A few more words of support, and he escorted her to the carriage.

Arriving at the Russian delegation party, Nikolai reminded himself to treat Annelisa as a man. Exiting the carriage, he waited on the sidewalk below but didn't extend his hand to help her down the stairs, despite the look of surprise she shot him.

"Come, Albert. We can't be late."

Annelisa stood on the top step waiting for him to help her, and he whispered, "I wouldn't give my hand to a man, Annelisa. Remember who you're supposed to be."

A look of recognition crossed her face and she whispered, "Oh," as she stepped down to the ground. "Nikolai, what if I forget? I've been a female for twenty-five years and a man for mere hours."

As they walked up the stairs of the stately home in front of them, Nikolai whispered instructions. "Try to lower your voice. And bow. Make sure your handshake is strong, but not too strong. And no giggling."

Annelisa turned to him and in a voice full of exasperation said, "I do not giggle, sir."

"Yes, you do. It's quite charming, in fact, especially when I'm making love to you. But as Albert, there is to be no giggling. Understand?"

"I don't giggle."

"Then that's one thing you won't have to worry about. Now when I introduce you to Count Borislav, shake his hand and say very little. If you can get by him, you should be all right."

"Please tell me that will be later, after I've had some time to practice, Nikolai. Please."

"No, you'll meet him first, as soon as we enter. Now let me see if your moustache is on properly."

Annelisa turned toward him and as he inspected above her lip, he took out his pocket watch to pretend to check the time. Looking down at the watch, he whispered, "I want to be inside you now more than you can know. Remember that as we do this."

Nikolai saw how his words aroused her. "Ready, Albert?"

Just as he'd said, they met his superior, Count Vladimir Borislav, immediately upon entering and Nikolai watched with pride as Annelisa did just as he'd instructed. Safely past the Count, they began to mingle with the partygoers, and with each introduction he saw Annelisa's confidence increase.

Alone for a moment, she turned to him and boasted, "This is much easier than I thought. These people actually think I'm a man."

"More than you think. But your greatest test is coming this way."

"Greatest test? I thought the Count was my greatest test."

Nikolai turned his attention to the two women coming toward them and mumbled, "No, these are."

Nikolai bowed and shot Annelisa a look to do the same, which she hurriedly did, before he began the introductions.

"Ladies, how wonderful to see you again. Let me introduce you to Albert Fielding. Albert, these charming ladies are the sisters, the Countesses Borislav, Olga and Yelena."

"It's a pleasure to meet you, Countesses."

Nikolai watched as the two women scanned Annelisa from head to toe and back again. When he'd said they'd be her greatest test, he hadn't meant there would be any problem convincing them she was a man. The Countesses Borislav would see trousers and a jacket and automatically accept her as a man. In fact, they'd accept the fact all too well.

Notorious libertines, they'd be quite interested in a new male to pursue. More correctly, Yelena would be interested in a new man. Olga had long chased after Nikolai, much to his chagrin. With her eyes that seemed at times to be so big as to make her resemble a bug and her all too ample breasts that always seemed to be spilling out of her dresses, Countess Olga Borislav was just another potential mate he hoped his family wouldn't insist he choose.

"Oh, Nikolai, he's wonderful. Where have you been hiding him?" Yelena asked as her sister fixed her eyes on his crotch as she always did when they met.

"He's the nephew of a business associate. I knew he'd enjoy himself here."

Yelena cooed her agreement and wrapped her hand around Annelisa's arm to move her prey to a more private location in the corner of the room a few feet away.

"Count? Don't we...aren't we..." Annelisa stammered in fear as Yelena pulled her toward her goal.

"Yelena, I'm going to need him back, so you can only have him for a few minutes."

Nikolai saw Annelisa's eyes grow wide in terror. "Albert, just a few minutes."

Fear raced through Annelisa's body as she was hauled off toward the corner of the room by this exceptionally eager woman. Damn, Nikolai! Why was he doing this? This woman obviously had designs on her—Albert—and planned to pursue them.

Once in the corner, the Countess began pawing at Annelisa's arms and neck, like an animal in heat. In no time, she saw the true horror of the situation. The woman wanted to kiss her!

"Countess Borislav, why don't we..." she began but was immediately cut off.

"Yelena. Call me Yelena, Albert."

Her sickeningly sweet voice, similar to her sister Olga's, nearly turned Annelisa's stomach.

"Very well, Yelena. Perhaps we can talk for a bit before we...do anything."

Before she knew it, Yelena had taken her hand and placed it just above the neckline of her dress, directly on the swell of her breast. Nearly panting from desire, her breasts rose and fell, nearly tumbling out of her dress with each inhale.

"What would you like to talk about, Albert?" With each word, her hands moved closer and closer to between Annelisa's legs.

Quickly, she grabbed her hands and held them tightly in hers. "Yelena, why don't you tell me how you know Nikolai."

Undeterred, she squeezed one of her hands out of Annelisa's grip and began stroking her forearm as she detailed how she and Olga knew Nikolai.

"Nikolai is an old friend of our family. He's also Russian nobility. And as I'm sure you can tell, he's very attracted to my sister. The feeling is mutual. In fact, I wouldn't be surprised if an announcement about their engagement came quite soon."

Annelisa directed her attention to Nikolai and Olga just feet away. She quickly assessed that the woman was wholly unappealing and was in serious need of a new dressmaker, even more so than Yelena. But Annelisa's focus was riveted to Nikolai's face, which seemed to indicate he liked being alone with her.

For the first time, jealousy spiked inside her as she watched him smile and even laugh as the horrid woman touched his chest while she flirted shamelessly with him. He was enjoying himself with her while she was trapped with Yelena and her eager hands.

Tearing the woman's hands from her coat, Annelisa marched over to them and announced, "It's time we left, Nikolai."

From behind her she heard Yelena whine about the hour being early, and for a moment it seemed like Nikolai would throw her back into her arms. Thankfully, he turned to Olga and bid his goodbyes before following Annelisa to say goodnight to their host.

But Yelena was not to be put off so easily. Almost tackling Annelisa from behind, she spun her around and kissed her on the lips, much to Annelisa's shock. "I do hope to see you again soon, Albert."

By the time she reached the front steps, Annelisa was in a rage, but she struggled to keep it under control.

Jealous over watching him with one sister and furious about being thrown as a bone to the other, she stormed toward the carriage only to find they must wait for it to arrive.

Nikolai walked at his usual leisurely pace, his long stride keeping close to her with little effort. As he joined her to wait for their carriage, he asked, "Did you have a pleasant time, Albert?"

"Don't speak to me."

"I thought you might enjoy the Countesses."

Annelisa turned to face him. "You knew they'd be here?"

"Of course. They attend all these diplomatic functions."

The anger began to grow in her to the point tears began to form in her eyes. He'd brought her here to see the woman he intended to marry. He'd brought his concubine to meet his future wife.

"I hate you!"

Then suddenly it dawned on her. Finally, a way out of their arrangement. If he were to marry Olga Borislav, then he couldn't blackmail her with the threat of telling her father what they'd done.

"I hope you'll be happy with the Countess. And now I've found a way to free myself from your blackmail."

"Happy with the Countess?"

"Yelena told me you are to be married. That means you can't threaten me with going to my father anymore."

The carriage pulled up in front of them, and Annelisa quickly got in and sat down. Nikolai joined her and as they began their trip home, he folded his arms across his chest.

"You're jealous. I'm flattered, Annelisa."

"Jealous? Absolutely not. Although I didn't take you for the type to like such a woman, I wish you well. I'm certainly not jealous."

"Yes, you are. But you have no reason to be. I will not be marrying Olga Borislav, no matter how much she wishes I would."

"I don't care."

"Then why are you so angry?"

"Why am I angry? You let that awful woman paw at me and she kissed me!"

In the dim light of the carriage, Annelisa saw Nikolai grin. Something in her snapped, and she lunged at him, arms swinging. He was much quicker and stronger and held her hands still as she continued to act out her anger.

"How could you?" she cried.

"Calm down. You'll hurt yourself."

As she wrestled against him, he pulled her onto his lap and forced her to sit down. When she continued to fight him, he warned, "Sit still or I swear I'll spank that pretty little bottom of yours."

Annelisa stilled, stunned into compliance. "You wouldn't."

"I will if you don't sit still. Don't say I didn't warn you."

Just as she was about to fight back, his lips were on hers kissing her more passionately than ever before. His tongue searched for hers, sending waves of pleasure straight to all the parts of her body she so desperately wished he'd kiss too. Mindless with anger, jealousy, and desire, she ground her body against his, begging for relief.

Throwing her hat across the carriage, Nikolai moved to her jacket and then her shirt, nearly tearing the buttons off as he worked to free her from it. His hands tore at her pants and he groaned, "Take them off. Now."

Desperate to be free of them and back on top of him, she wriggled out of her pants as Nikolai stripped his off to show his cock fully erect and ready. Wearing only her open shirt, she eagerly climbed onto his lap and slid up and down his cock, coating him with her juices.

"Remember when I told you I wanted to be inside you? I couldn't think of anything else all night. Only your wet cunt wrapped around my cock."

While he spoke, he thrust his hips off the seat, sliding through her slick folds as she wished he would just find the mark and bury himself deeply inside her.

She needed an answer first, though.

"Even when you were talking to that woman?"

"I didn't hear a word she said. The whole time she was talking, I was watching to see if you were all right and fantasizing about this. Didn't you see the smile on my face?"

Annelisa didn't know why, but his answer pleased her almost as much as what they were about to do. And she didn't understand exactly why that pleased her either.

Nikolai loved that Annelisa had been jealous. As she writhed around on his lap, alternately teasing him and then almost begging to be fucked, he watched her beautiful face register the emotions she felt, its loveliness not even obscured by the moustache and men's wig she wore.

In these intimate moments, she was so open, but he knew as soon as they were out of each other's arms, she'd return to denying her feelings for him. A twinge of anger bit at him, and he roughly yanked the moustache off her skin.

"Nikolai! That hurt!"

Immediately guilty, he whispered, "Let me make it better, love," and began tenderly flicking his tongue over the sensitive skin.

"Please don't tease me. I don't think I can handle it tonight."

Lifting her up, he found what he'd fantasized about for hours and slowly filled her until his cock was completely inside her.

"No more teasing, moya milaya."

For a moment, he was still, the motion of the carriage delivering the incredible sensations they both experienced. Her eyes looked into his, and for that moment she wasn't the Annelisa who complained about her time with him. She was the Annelisa who was completely his, body and soul.

He'd have to wait for her mind, but he'd take her

body and soul for now.

"Ride me, Annelisa. Show me how much you want me."

He half expected her to demand he show her how much he wanted her, which he would gladly have obliged, but instead he was pleasantly surprised when she began to fuck him with abandon. Her mouth sought out his, and he gave her everything she needed.

As her body crept closer to the edge, she whimpered his name against his lips, like a single word plea for him to show her how much he wanted her. Each time made him thrust deeper to touch that spot that gave her what she so desperately wanted.

She tightened around him and began to milk his cock toward his own release. There, in the dim light of the carriage as they rode toward home, she shuddered as her release took her over and his sent his seed deep into her. Exhausted, she laid her head on his shoulder and wrapped her arms around him.

For Nikolai, this was the closeness that came from his love for her. Making love—fucking—whatever they did was an extension of his feelings. He believed she loved him too, but as he sat there in the carriage, still joined with her and her holding him, he knew the spell would be broken as soon as he released her.

What would it take to make her admit her feelings?

Ten

Nikolai lay in bed drowsily thinking of his last time with Annelisa. Despite being less than two days earlier, the event seemed to want to fade from his memory, and he fought to relive the sweetness of their rendezvous.

God, she excited him! Just the thought of her riding him in their carriage, her passion in control of her, made him hard now. Even more, though, he wished she'd want to be with him as he wanted her.

Because no matter how many times she begged him not to stop while they made love, he knew she still regarded their time together as a means to an end.

Stroking his chin, he thought about how he could make her come to him. He didn't mind continuing their arrangement, but in truth, he knew it couldn't go on indefinitely. Hell, she may even be carrying his child at that moment, so their agreement would have to change to one of marriage. But he wanted her to want him, not out of obligation but out of love.

"Uprymaya," he grumbled as he closed his eyes in frustration.

It was unlikely she would admit she'd grown to care for him, even if she in fact had. Her independent streak was far too powerful to let feelings get in the way. No, if he ever wanted Annelisa to love him enough to admit it, he'd need something more than just giving her physical pleasure.

What she needs is a dose of her own medicine.

He'd told her to return that day, so if he intended to put a plan into motion, there was no better time than the present. When she arrived that afternoon, he'd begin the work needed to finally have her as his.

A pounding on the front door interrupted his thoughts, and he hurriedly got dressed. By the time he'd reached the main floor, his manservant had let a very upset Maksim in and he was frantically pacing through Nikolai's parlor, wringing his hands.

"Maksim, what brings you here so early this morning?" he asked as he took a seat on the settee.

"Nikolai, it's the worst news! There has been an attempt on the Tsar's life!"

Immediately, Nikolai stood and asked, "What do we know? Has he survived?"

"Yes, thank God! What has the world become, Nikolai?"

While Maksim fretted over the state of affairs in modern Russia, Nikolai rejoiced that his Tsar had survived yet another assassination attempt. This wouldn't be the last, though, he was sure. Alexander II's reign had introduced many changes to his beloved country – many changes that made discontent all the more possible. But for the moment, he was thankful the Tsar was safe.

Maksim handed Nikolai a letter. "This came for you at the office."

Nikolai read the message with a sense of regret. He'd been ordered to return home to deal with the implications of the attempt on the Tsar's life and was to leave immediately.

"Maksim, I've been called back to Russia. While I'm gone, I need you to continue our work with the members of Parliament who favor our ideas. Also, I'll be sending dispatches I'll need you to deliver to a number of people I've been meeting with."

"Of course, Nikolai. I'll be sure to keep you abreast of everything happening here."

Nikolai knew Maksim wouldn't be able to inform him of the most important person to him in England. Quickly, he realized he'd need to pay a visit to her father before he left and hope he could get a free moment to speak to her.

"Maksim, I need to make one stop before I leave. Arrange a coach for me. I'll only be a short time and I'll leave upon my return."

"I'll get to it immediately," Maksim said and left to make the necessary arrangements.

Nine a.m. was exceedingly early to be paying a visit to

anyone, but as Nikolai pounded on the Fieldings' front door, he didn't care. He just hoped Annelisa would be available to talk.

The Fieldings' butler opened the door and stuck his head through the crack. "Sir?"

"I apologize for the hour, but I need to see your master."

The servant opened the door and stood aside for Nikolai to pass. "Of course, Count Shetkolov. If you'll wait here, I'll fetch Mr. Fielding immediately."

Nikolai watched the man hurry to the breakfast room and hoped Annelisa was there to hear him announce his arrival. Only a few minutes later, Andrew Fielding came out to greet him in the hallway.

"To what do I owe the pleasure of a visit on this morning, my friend?"

"May I speak to you in private, Andrew?"

Nodding, Andrew placed his hand on Nikolai's back to guide him to the study. "Of course, Nikolai. Is everything all right?"

As Andrew closed the door behind them, Nikolai explained the reason for his visit. Andrew sat behind his desk, his fingers steepled in front of him. "I'm sorry to hear of the attempt on the Tsar's life, Nikolai. How long will you be gone?"

"I don't know. But please know I have Maksim monitoring our friends and foes in Parliament. If you need to get a message to me, know you can trust him."

"Don't worry, friend. Take care of your man and be safe. These are troubled times, I'm afraid."

Nikolai extended his hand. "Thank you, Andrew. I'll be sure to see you when I return. And if you could keep this news between us, I'd appreciate it."

As he left the study, he spied Annelisa standing in the doorway that led to the breakfast room, her face the picture of concern. He moved his head slightly to let her know to follow him outside and hoped she'd understand his signal.

Nikolai needn't have worried. Before he made it down the front steps, she was at his side peppering him with questions.

"What did you have to speak to my father about so early this morning? What could you have to discuss?"

"Someone attempted to assassinate Tsar Alexander this morning. I've been recalled to Russia."

Annelisa's gaze left his face, and she looked down at the ground. "I'm sorry, Nikolai. Is he going to be all right?"

"I believe so, but as a diplomat, I have to help ensure his reign continues to prosper."

"How long will you be gone?"

Nikolai swore he heard her voice hitch as she asked. "I don't know. Is that sadness in your voice?"

Immediately defensive, Annelisa's eyes grew wide. "That's ridiculous. I just wondered how long my reprieve from your blackmail would be. That's all."

Nikolai studied her face for the truth. How much she would miss him could be seen in her eyes, which seemed on the verge of tears.

Maybe she did care.

"Well, I pledge to continue my heartfelt efforts to ensure you never suffer from hysteria as soon as I return, Annelisa. In the meantime, I'll be pleased to remember how much you despise marriage and trust you won't choose another in my absence."

Annelisa smiled. "Like I would be so foolish as to allow myself to become involved in a relationship with another man."

Nikolai began walking to his coach but turned around to look at her. "A relationship? Well, I promise that when I return it will be just that. I told you before that you won't get rid of me that easily."

Chuckling, she said, "As if I could ever be that lucky. Have a safe trip, Nikolai,"

As he rode away, he looked back to see her still standing there watching him leave. He was convinced more than ever that she cared. Now all he had to do was find a way to make her admit it.

Annelisa was torn between a feeling of victory over being freed from her arrangement with Nikolai and missing him as she watched his coach roll away from the house. The feeling of victory was short-lived as she admitted to herself that what had begun as blackmail had grown into a relationship. That she'd as much as admitted it to him just minutes before unnerved her, though.

She'd mastered the art of keeping men away, but to make one love her? That was a distinctly different story. He seemed to have some interest in her. He had, in fact, wanted to marry her when he'd found out about Violet's true identity.

But that had been out of obligation.

As the last sight of him faded from view, she turned to walk back to the house. For the first time in her life, the thought of trading her freedom for the love of a man crossed her mind.

Her thoughts filled with Nikolai, she made her way toward the stairs to go to her room, but her father caught her before she made it.

"Annelisa, come in to my study, please."

Since her stunt the night of the ball and her subsequent refusal to name the man who'd taken her virginity, their relationship had been at best strained. And now with Thornton Sutcliffe's blackmail, Annelisa felt worse than ever and so wished she and her father could return to the relationship they'd always had.

Her father sat in a chair near the fireplace and called to her to take a seat next to him. Unsure of what he could want to discuss with her, she sat down and waited for him to begin, her gaze settled on her lap.

For a long time, he said nothing, but when he finally spoke, his voice was the same as it had been before their recent problems.

"Annelisa, I don't know why you did what you did, but for what it's worth, I'm glad you won't be marrying the Earl of Swindon."

Looking up, she saw the face of the man who'd taken care of her for so long and she wanted to cry for all she'd put him through. Reaching over, she wrapped her arms around his neck and hugged him tightly.

"Thank you, Father. I'm so sorry what I've done has created such a mess for you. I never meant for any of it to hurt you."

Annelisa sat back in her chair and wiped her eyes. She'd waited so long to tell him how she felt, and the warm smile that met her words touched her heart.

"If you're referring to that scoundrel Sutcliffe, don't worry. Your father didn't get to where he is today without learning how to deal with the Thornton Sutcliffes of this world. I'm more concerned about you, dear."

Annelisa saw the concern in her father's eyes. "Oh, don't worry about me. As long as I know you understand why I didn't want to marry him, I can deal with whatever he does. I'm a lot like my father that way."

"I'm not worried about that, dear. I'm talking about your future."

"Please don't worry. I'll be fine."

"I just worry about you. Other girls are already married with children at your age. I know you're modern, but what will happen if you don't marry?"

Sure she wanted at the very least to calm his fears, Annelisa took his hands in hers. "I never said I wouldn't marry, Father. Just that I wanted to marry someone of my choosing who I love."

Andrew Fielding's face brightened. "That puts me at ease somewhat, dear, but do you have anyone in mind?"

Annelisa shook her head and smiled. "No, but don't give up on me yet. Perhaps there's a man out there who could love me."

"He'd be a lucky man, Annelisa. You have many gifts to offer the right man."

"Thank you, Father."

Rising from his seat, he said, "Time for you to go. I have work to attend to. But there's one more thing. There's no need to be sad over Nikolai's leaving. He'll be back."

The blood rushed to her face, and she was sure her blush gave away far more than she'd prefer concerning her feelings for Nikolai. "Why would I be sad?"

"I've seen you two talking recently. He's a count, you know."

"Yes, I know," she said with a smile. "More matchmaking, Father?"

"Just food for thought, dear."

Annelisa left the study before her father had the chance to continue the discussion. Walking to her room, she chuckled at the idea of her father innocently thinking of Nikolai as a potential suitor.

"Annelisa, where have you been?"

Turning, she saw Cecile coming toward her from her room. Her face told her she had something on her mind.

"With Father in his study."

Catching up to her, Cecile pushed Annelisa into her room.

"Cecile, what are you doing?"

Before she knew it, Cecile had pushed her down onto the bed and stood glaring at her.

"Annelisa Fielding, you lied to me!"

Her mind racing to determine which lie her sister

referred to, Annelisa quickly decided playing dumb was a far better plan than blindly choosing a lie and defending herself.

"Cecile, I have no idea what you're talking about. Calm down."

"I thought you trusted me. How could you have kept it from me?"

If she didn't get Cecile to lower her voice, everyone in the house would soon know what she meant. Taking her hand, Annelisa brought her sister to the bed and pulled her to sit with her.

"Please sit down. I promise we can talk about whatever you'd like. Just keep your voice down."

"How could you not tell me about your times with Count Shetkolov?" Cecile asked with a hurt look on her face. "I thought we told one another everything."

"How did you know?"

"I saw you leaving his house. What's going on? I thought you didn't like him."

"I never said I didn't like him, Cecile. He's an intelligent and honorable man."

"You said you weren't interested in him. That his good looks didn't matter to you."

"They didn't and I wasn't."

"Then what changed to make you go to his house without anyone else? What did the two of you do?"

Annelisa lifted her eyebrows in disbelief at her sister's naiveté. "Cecile, you really need to read those books in my bottom drawer. You're going to be married soon and need to know about what a man and woman do together."

Annelisa had hoped this would deter her sister's questioning, but she had no such luck. Cecile was not to be put off this time.

"Oh, no you don't, Annelisa. I'm not interested in talking about my future. I want to know what's going on with Nikolai and no more lying."

Annelisa stood up and began pacing back and forth across the room. To be honest, she was almost relieved to tell someone of her secret.

"Nikolai figured out it was me at the ball and offered to do the honorable thing and marry me. I declined his offer and he threatened to tell father everything. To make sure he didn't, I told him I'd do anything. So..."

"So you go to his house and have sex with him?"

Annelisa stopped pacing and turned toward her sister. "We make love, Cecile."

"Do you love him then?"

Cecile's question hung in the air like a huge question mark over Annelisa's head. Did she love him?

"Well?"

"I don't know."

After the words left her mouth, she exhaled and dropped her shoulders, as if the words had been a burden she was finally free of at last.

"I don't understand you, Annelisa. You didn't like the earl because he was odious, but now you don't know how you feel about Nikolai, even though he's very handsome, successful, and you've been sneaking off to be with him?"

"It's more complicated than that. I don't know how he feels about me. He's never asked me to marry him again. What if he just wants me for sex?"

"Have you let him know you care for him?"

Annelisa silently shook her head.

"Then tell him."

"I can't. He's been recalled to Russia, and I don't know when he'll return."

Cecile stood up and wrapped her arms around her sister. "Then tell him when he gets back before another woman falls in love with those gorgeous blue eyes and steals him away forever."

Eleven

Annelisa waited in her father's study, her toes tapping the floor nervously in anticipation of Nikolai's arrival. His three week absence would end in mere minutes if his cable was correct, and her excitement at seeing him was nearly killing her.

To her surprise, the time away from him had only made her feelings increase, and she longed to see him again. She would take Cecile's advice and confess her feelings to him with the desperate hope that he cared for her in return.

Unable to sit still, she stood and walked to the window to look out at the garden. The memory of her refusal of his marriage proposal in that very garden made her wince. She'd been so cavalier that day.

Please let him be better than I was when I tell him how I feel.

"Andrew, how are you my friend?"

Nikolai's accent hit her deep inside, and she turned to see him standing in the doorway to the study. Her eyes traveled over his face and body, from his blue eyes and his goatee that made him seem so foreign and exotic, to his coat and trousers that covered the body she'd missed for the past three weeks.

"And Miss Fielding. What a lovely surprise to see you."

As Nikolai and her father moved to sit, Annelisa stood frozen to the spot in fear. Everything she hadn't been sure of bombarded her brain, nearly overwhelming her.

She couldn't deny it any longer. She loved him. But did he love her?

Annelisa watched as he and her father talked about the Tsar's safety and Nikolai's return to England. In truth, she only heard a fraction of their conversation as the sound of her heart's pounding seemed to drown out much in the room.

"You must be happy to be back, Nikolai. I know I'm happy to have you back so our plans for my company's expansion in Russia can commence."

"I'm pleased to be back, but I won't be staying long before I return once again to Russia."

Annelisa stepped forward. "Oh? Why?"

"I have wonderful news. I am to return home to marry the Countess Stravinsky in one week. I'll return to my post after the wedding, so don't worry, Andrew. Your plans will happen."

"Congratulations, Nikolai. This is wonderful news!"

As her father professed his happiness at Nikolai's impending marriage, Annelisa felt like the room was spinning around her. Married? Her Nikolai was marrying some Russian countess? Cecile had been right. Some other woman had fallen in love with those beautiful blue eyes and stolen him away from her.

As she stood there watching the man she loved beaming about marrying another woman, her stomach turned and she felt like she was going to be sick. Suddenly, there didn't seem to be enough air in the room and the dress she'd worn especially because he'd liked it before seemed like it would smother her.

Tears welled up in her eyes as the emotional disappointment enveloped her.

She'd lost him.

Before she began crying, Annelisa said, "Please excuse me, Father. I feel ill. Congratulations, sir," and quickly exited the room.

In the hallway, she stood with her back pressed against the wall, afraid that without the support, she'd collapse. As her father told Nikolai about Thornton Sutcliffe's blackmail, tears rolled down over her cheeks. Her Nikolai was another woman's.

For days Annelisa stayed in bed, truly sick over Nikolai's impending marriage to some countess whose name she couldn't remember. Cecile tried to console her, but little could be done. Finally, she suggested the impossible.

"Annelisa, you must tell him how you feel. Even if he

still marries Countess What's-Her-Name, he'll know you truly cared for him."

Her head buried in a pillow, Annelisa said, "He doesn't care for me, Cecile. Why would he care how I feel about him?"

"He might not, but you say he's an honorable man. He should know."

"He's not an honorable man! He never cared for me. He only used me until he found a suitable woman to marry!"

Cecile pulled her sister from the pillow. "Do you honestly believe that? Do you honestly believe he never cared at all?"

Annelisa wasn't sure what she believed. She'd made such a mess of everything, and now the one man she'd ever wanted to marry was marrying another woman.

"I don't know what I believe, Cecile. All I know is that I've lost him."

An hour later, with a great deal of help from Cecile, including the knowledge that he was in his neighborhood home that day, Annelisa set off for Nikolai's house one last time. She would tell him how she felt and hoped it at least make her feel better.

Something told her it would have the exact opposite effect.

As she made her way over the country road, a thought she'd never had before repeated in her head. Annelisa Fielding—spinster. For the first time, the idea that she'd be alone settled into her brain and tormented her. Worse was the knowledge that she'd be alone because of her own actions. Nikolai had asked her to marry him and she'd refused.

Why had she been so foolish?

Nikolai watched Annelisa through the front window as she stood at the edge of his property for what seemed like hours. He'd waited for days to see her since he hadn't had a chance to speak to her that day at her house, and his heart ached as he looked at the sad face she wore. It had taken all his diplomatic powers of persuasion to convince her sister to tell Annelisa to visit him, but there was no other way to get to see her, especially after he'd heard she was sick in bed for days.

He watched her finally make her move toward the house and then heard her soft knock at the door. When he opened it, he felt his heart miss a beat. She looked so sad.

"Come in."

Annelisa walked past him into the parlor, which still remained almost entirely empty without most of the furniture. With no seating choices, she sat down on the settee and he took his position next to her.

She remained silent, her eyes fixed on her folded hands in her lap, looking nothing like the Annelisa he'd known.

"I'm so happy you came, Annelisa."

Suddenly, the dam broke.

"Are you? Why? Why are you marrying another woman? I thought you cared for me. Was what we did merely physical? If it was, why did you ask me to marry you?"

Nikolai couldn't help but smile. This was the Annelisa he remembered.

"One question at a time. Yes, I am happy you came. I missed you. And what we did was never merely physical, not from the first time we were together at the masquerade ball. And I asked you to marry me because it was the honorable thing to do when I found out it was you I'd made love to that night."

Tears welled up in her eyes. "You didn't love me. It was just an obligation."

"No, I didn't love you when I asked you to marry me. I believed we could grow to love one another, but you didn't want to marry me."

Annelisa sniffled and stood to leave. "I have to go. I can't do this. I hope you'll be happy. Goodbye, Nikolai."

As she started to move past him, he grabbed her arm and yanked her down onto his lap. Stunned, she stared at him, her eyes wide with confusion.

"Uprymaya. Why does everything have to be a fight with you, Annelisa?"

"What are you doing? Let me go right now. You're engaged to someone else. Why would you tease me like this?"

Nikolai put his finger up to her mouth to silence her. "For once, I want you to listen without saying a word. I love you, Annelisa. I've loved you since that night in the Stewarts' garden. But I knew you didn't love me, and even when I believed you'd grown to feel something for me, I knew you wouldn't admit it."

"What are you saying?"

"There is no Countess Stravinsky I'm marrying. I mean, there is a countess with that name, but she's my mother's age and happily married to the Count Stravinsky."

Annelisa sat staring at him, stunned by his words. "Why did you lie? You broke my heart!"

Nikolai gently caressed her damp cheek. "I'm sorry. I needed a way to make you admit your feelings for me."

Leaping off his lap, Annelisa glared in anger at him. "How could you do that? I was sick in bed for days over you!"

He tried to pull her back to him, but she was already on her way to the door. Quickly, he caught her and held her to him as she struggled against his body.

"Annelisa, stop. I just told you I love you and I'm not marrying anyone else."

"Days, Nikolai! I was in bed for days thinking I'd lost you to another woman!"

Taking her face in his hands, he kissed her lips and whispered against them, "I love you, Annelisa. And I love that you cared enough to be sad for days when you thought you'd lost me."

"Ya tebya lyublyu," she whispered back.

Nikolai beamed at the words "I love you" in his own language coming from the woman he adored.

"Moya milaya."

"You always say that to me. I was so determined to

find out how to tell you I love you in Russian that I never found out what that means."

As he began removing her dress, he whispered, "It means, 'my sweet'."

Annelisa smiled. "I love you, Nikolai. I was devastated at the thought of losing you. You're the only man I've ever loved."

As she made her confession, he slid her dress down over her hips and let it puddle on the floor at her feet.

"Not to worry. As I told you that day I asked you to marry me, you won't get rid of me that easily."

He made quick work of her stockings and undergarments while he planted soft kisses over her stomach. When she was finally completely undressed, he looked up at her to see her watching him with almost frightened eyes.

"Annelisa?"

Twisting her face into a worried expression, she said quietly, "Every time I've ever been with you has been an act. I don't know..."

Nikolai rose to kiss her on the lips. Smiling, he answered, "I know, but I love this Annelisa, not Violet or you as Albert or even the Annelisa everyone else sees."

When he'd finished unbuttoning his shirt and pants, he slid out of them and stepped back to look at the woman he adored. Slowly, he trailed his fingertips over her skin, lingering on her nipples as they hardened under his touch.

"Nikolai..."

"No more talking. Let me show you what I've thought of every day since I last saw you."

Nikolai swept her up in his arms, and for the first time, took her up to his bedroom instead of that lone couch in the parlor. They made love as he knew they always would—openly and sweetly, with no masks or façade to shield either of them.

Afterward, as Annelisa rested her head on his chest, Nikolai thought about how he was going to tell his friend and future father-in-law he wanted to marry his daughter. He also thought about his talk with Thornton Sutcliffe earlier that day.

"Annelisa, I spoke to the Earl of Swindon today. He's been blackmailing your father, but I don't think he'll be doing that anymore."

"Good. It broke my heart to hear him say the things he did to him, and I told him what I thought of him to his face."

"You told the earl this?"

Annelisa sat up. "Yes, I did. I don't care who you noblemen think you are. It's not right to blackmail people. That goes for you too."

"Does it now? Well, I wouldn't have had to blackmail you if you'd said yes the first time I asked you to marry me."

"Correction, Count. The only time you've asked me."

Nikolai smiled at the most stubborn woman he'd ever met. "You're right. And I even bent down on one knee and you said no. I guess if I ever ask again, it would have to be something even bigger."

Quietly, she said, "Well, maybe not. It's the thought that counts. Perhaps you should try it again and see if it goes better this time."

Nikolai shook his head and frowned. "And I'd have to get permission to marry anyone other than Russian nobility, so that could take some time, if it ever happened."

Annelisa put her head down and sighed. "I understand."

"Thankfully, I had to return home just recently and received permission then."

When she looked up, Nikolai saw the look of surprise on her face. "Will you marry me, Annelisa Fielding?"

Annelisa fell on top of him and hugged him tightly as she said the words he'd longed to hear since that day in the garden. "Yes, yes, I'll marry you, Nikolai."

"And you want a husband now?"

"I don't know if I want a husband, but I want you. If that means I get a husband, then a husband I'll have."

Later, as they lay in bed together, Annelisa asked, "How did you convince the earl to stop blackmailing my father, Nikolai?"

"I threatened him."

Annelisa looked up at him. "That doesn't seem very diplomatic."

"He wasn't dealing with a diplomat. He was dealing with a man in love."

Snuggling up to him, she said, "I certainly hope if we ever have a son, he's just like you. But if we have a daughter, I want her to be just like me."

Nikolai kissed the top of her head. "God help me, let it be a boy. No amount of diplomacy would help me with two of you."

The End

Look for *Love's Master*,
another Gabrielle Bisset novella
set in Victorian England!

EXCERPT

Lily sat with the newspaper in her lap, praying that someone new could be found among the advertisers she'd already been forced to dismiss as possibilities. A fitful night's sleep tossing and turning while her mind raced over having to meet Captain Danvers caused her nerves to be on edge, and she was embarrassed to admit she dreaded William's impending arrival in the breakfast room. Desperate to find a new nanny or tutor, she buried her nose in the paper and began what she hoped would be a fruitful search.

The advertisements offered nothing, and as she sat dejected, she turned to the Agony Column, knowing at least she'd find kindred spirits in the lost lovers and desperate souls searching for that which life and circumstance had taken or failed to provide.

Even a brief perusal of the notices in this part of the Times provided a reader a glimpse into the often lonely world of the strangers who inhabited London and its suburbs. With any luck, Lily hoped to get lost in the world of these strangers so as to forget the one she'd been thrust into and which seemed to offer only one way out: marriage to a certain Captain Danvers.

As the chaos of the day began with William's appearance at breakfast, she strived to block it out, focusing instead on the suffering of those outside the house. The column was a particularly long one, with notices of long lost relatives urgently seeking their family members and lovers conveying the details of their illicit meetings. She came upon the last advertisement and her heart skipped a beat in excitement. Worried she'd misread it, she read it again.

"K. is a strict disciplinarian and not afraid of a rather unruly pupil."

Could it be? Had she found a tutor for William? As she attempted to ignore his stomping and temper tantrum over his mother's timid request he finish his oatmeal, Lily read and reread the notice, her anticipation building at the thought of someone finally disciplining the child properly.

"Elizabeth," she said as he stormed out of the room to abuse the cook, "how would one find a person who advertised in the Agony Column?"

Her sister-in-law looked relieved at the idea of discussing other people's distress. "I don't know for sure, but you would likely have to advertise a reply."

Lily almost leaped from her chair, thrilled by the prospect of hiring William's newest tutor—a strict disciplinarian!

"Elizabeth, please have John arrange the carriage for me. I'm going into town."

As the carriage rolled toward London, the steady rhythm of the horses' hooves hitting the road relaxed Lily. Closing her eyes, she shut out everything but the sound and allowed herself to fantasize about the mysterious stranger she hoped would soon bring calm and order to the house.

My mid-morning she'd placed her reply to the potential tutor and was on her way back home. As her carriage pulled up to the house, she congratulated herself on being such a take charge woman. Her triumph was cut short, however, by the vision of Mason Danvers she spied through the carriage window. Taking a deep breath, she resigned herself to the fact that what she'd dreaded had begun. As he helped her out of the carriage, she felt his gaze roam over her. Ever the military man, he was surveying the prize he sought to capture and devising a plan of attack, she thought to herself.

"Miss Scott, how are you today?"

Lily immediately felt irritated by his negation of her three years of marriage. Pretending he was a stranger, she asked in an indignant tone that was only partially false, "Do we know each other, sir?" as she haughtily took back her hand.

Bowing, he said, "Pardon me, dear lady. I understand you may not remember me as I do you, but I'm here at your brother's request. I'm Captain Mason Danvers. Please let me escort you into the house."

Lily looked at the man her brother had chosen for her intended. As appealing as she remembered, he appeared to be genuinely interested in her, she realized to her surprise.

"Thank you, Captain. That's very nice of you," she answered more politely than genuinely.

She let him take her hand once more and felt the strength of his hand press gently against her skin. The power he possessed seemed to exude from his very pores, and she decided perhaps she should try to like him.

The problem was just as his every movement seemed to convey a very attractive strength, his speech conveyed a far less attractive overconfidence at times that she found more and more distasteful.

"Richard, I look forward to discussing that business deal with you. I believe I can help you as much as you may help me."

Lily watched as he strutted into the parlor with her brother. Her first real meeting with Captain Mason Danvers had left her with mixed feelings for him. True, he seemed to have some fine qualities, but as she watched him staring at her from an entire room away, she sensed she was the business deal he'd wanted to discuss.

Well, if he thinks closing this deal will be easy, he's definitely overestimated himself.

About the Author

K.M. Scott writes sexy contemporary romance with characters her readers love. A New York Times and USA Today bestselling author, she's been in love with romance since reading her first romance novel in junior high (she was a very curious girl!). Under her Gabrielle Bisset name, she also writes erotic historical and paranormal romance. She lives in Pennsylvania with her teenage son and a herd of animals and when she's not writing can be found reading or feeding her TV addiction.

Be sure to visit K.M.'s Facebook page at **https://www.facebook.com/kmscottauthor** for all the latest on her books, along with giveaways and other goodies! And to hear all the news on K.M. Scott books first, sign up for her newsletter today and be sure to visit her website at **http://www.kmscottbooks.com**

Visit Gabrielle's Facebook page and her website at: **http://www.gabriellebisset.com/** to find out about her books too!

Books by K.M. SCOTT:

Crash Into Me **(Heart of Stone #1)**
Fall Into Me **(Heart of Stone #2)**
Give In To Me **(Heart of Stone #3)**
The Heart of Stone Trilogy Box Set
Ever After **(A Heart of Stone Novella)**
A Heart of Stone Christmas

Temptation **(Club X #1)**
Surrender **(Club X #2)**
Possession **(Club X #3)**
Satisfaction **(Club X #4) COMING SOON!**

Silk **(Volume One)**
Silk **(Volume Two)**
Silk **(Volume Three)**
Silk **(Volume Four)**

Books by Gabrielle Bisset:

Vampire Dreams Revamped **(A Sons of Navarus Prequel)**
Blood Avenged **(Sons of Navarus #1)**
Blood Betrayed **(Sons of Navarus #2)**
Longing **(A Sons of Navarus Short Story)**
Blood Spirit **(Sons of Navarus #3)**
The Deepest Cut **(A Sons of Navarus Short Story)**
Blood Prophecy **(Sons of Navarus #4)**
Blood & Dreams Sons of Navarus Box Set
Love's Master
Masquerade
The Victorian Erotic Romance Trilogy

www.ingramcontent.com/pod-product-compliance
Lightning Source LLC
Chambersburg PA
CBHW030231180626
46810CB00008B/3071

* 9 7 8 1 9 4 1 5 9 4 1 9 3 *